Frank

Antoinette,
"Accidents make people's"

Joseph Gibbs

Frank

ISBNs:
978-0-9861829-0-7 (print)
978-0-9861829-1-4 (eBook)

Brogancamden.com

For,
N.E.

YOU COULD SAY it began with the letters.

November 1984.

Dear Brogan,

You are thirteen now, which means you are well into a life that really is not going to give a good goddamn whether you are ready for it or not. Remember this, you're going to find out what that thing is for between your legs, and when you do, understand this! Use it as much as you can! Trust me! And when you learn what the hell it's for, remember, accidents make people! Get it? If not, look it up.

Happy Birthday,
Love, Frank.

Uncle Frank's birthday card arrived every year around Thanksgiving with a personal check that I wasn't allowed to cash (Will and Linda, my parents, knew full well that there wouldn't be any money in the account). His handwriting was a madman's scrawl, the uneven letters with their sharp arcs which would suddenly plummet into nonsensical and disjointed shapes like looking at a picture of an erratic frequency; the way that the lines of cursive went up and down in stabbing shards; the way that his letter "K" jabbed upward and downward like a pitchforked scream of just urgency. And somehow through that scribbled mess of words - I could hear him, a man that I had never met or spoken to, a gruff and cigarette scarred enunciation.

I kept the letters, with their gasoline scent. I saved the uncashed checks. I saved the envelopes that were stamped in Puerto Rico (which may have been on the moon as far as I was concerned). They found a suitable space in the bottom left-hand drawer of my desk, a dark and hidden cave of mystery, far from my mother's eye.

"Frank acts like an orangutan," Linda complained.

"I understand," Will said.

"Then don't let Brogan read the cards anymore."

"Okay."

They had caught me in the bathroom, naked, in front of the mirror, looking at my thirteen-year-old crotch. I forgot to lock the door. I must have been in there for some time when I saw the reflections of my parents in the mirror.

"No more letters," Linda said to Will, as if he were to blame.

"Pull your goddamn pants up boy," Will said.

I had never met Uncle Frank. In truth, he should have meant nothing. Frank never actually came to Thanksgiving dinner. He never came to the family Christmas party. He never acknowledged another's birthday. Those same letters always came whether Frank was in jail, drunk, out of sorts, or missing. Missing so often that my father nicknamed him "The Phantom." It suited Frank. He was a force heard, seldom seen, elusive, like a malevolent ghost - rattling chains in his cryptic letters through fitful and prophetic cursive.

IT WAS LATE November in the year that I would turn eighteen years old. The school year had aged, and the season brought another Thanksgiving. The autumn trees had changed from green to oranges and red, and then to the simple naked branches of the coming winter. The rain came for a time in the late fall, and the grounds were wet and muddy. Beyond the football field at Seton Preparatory High School, the once thick growth was now bare, revealing the "hidden lake" which was just past the school perimeter. That day I took another walk out to the lake again before class. The mud caked my shoes and kicked up brown onto my school slacks. A light rain should have made the walk miserable, but instead - it was pleasant with the drumming sound on my slicker.

My eye was still pretty sore. The bluish and purple meat just beneath that eye was just starting to heal. I had taken a pretty good left hook from Chaz Anderson that had connected just right. The cool wind felt good. My right hand was still stiff and swollen and the scabs were cracked and still bled, threatening my white shirt. I had gotten in a few good but effectively useless shots of my own during the quick fight. I unsuccessfully tried to make a fist. I put my hand in the ice-cold lake.

It wasn't much of a lake, more like a small retaining pond, and now the rain made a thousand impressions on the water. Spent cigarette butts were piled in white sticks from the fall season when the trees were still thick, and the students could smoke undetected. I still had a secluded view from behind the trees. The yellow school buses unloaded the freshmen students and despite the miserable weather, the winter track team still made their laps around the football field in the morning.

Seton Prep had the venerable feel of a New England town. Narrow tree-lined paths led to strong stone buildings with high cupolas and arched doorways with clenched jaws. They seemed ancient and immutable in the cold autumn morning, as if they had been there for a hundred years, secured and likely to be there for another hundred. Even the gymnasium, where the track team was now marching into single file, was a solid, windowless stone building, a relic of the Puritan North. Though it was a Catholic school, it seemed the Chapel did not belong: a modern and white-faced fraud rising against the contemptible grey northern sky, separate and out of place, like a tumor.

Brother Big had instructed me to meet him there this morning. It was getting near that time.

Inside, the halls of Seton Prep had the combined scent of close-bodied sweat of unwashed school blazers, the dusty heat that rose from the dormant radiators, and the musty and damp smell of a library. I only noticed it now because I knew that I would be leaving soon. Unlike the other seniors, I couldn't find anything miraculous or even touching about leaving. I looked for things to miss.

I wouldn't miss any of my classmates. That was the crazy part. Not one of them. Not even one of my teachers. Most of the faculty, if they hadn't quite crossed into batshit crazy land, had checked out some time ago. Dressed in mildewed suits, they were uninspired soldiers of a dated system spouting out commands while knowing in their hearts that the battle had already been lost. I guess it was the low pay that they received with the knowledge that a year's tuition at the school was about as much as a new car. Or maybe it was simply that the students here were mostly legacy, and their families were loaded, and they were mostly just pricks.

If I really had to find something to miss, anything, there was the cafeteria woman, timeless and ancient with her gray and silvery hair and her glassy eyes that were two different colors. She always looked up while handing over the change for your bagel. One day she had a bandage with tape over the top in the crook of her elbow, and the bandage had a rising dot of blood, and her blue ropey veins were rising beneath her tracing paper skin.

I thought about her sometimes, and I suppose that was missing someone. I looked for her when she didn't show up one day. She was invisible to the rest of the world. I imagined she was once a part of something somewhere in her own life, but now she was just a robot, catering to the imbecile children of Seton Prep, taking dollars and making change. In my mind I called her the Gray Lady. Once she had made a comment about Hamlet, which was tucked under my arm. "Not even Shakespeare was perfect," she said. "Ophelia was not a round character." The Gray Lady had come to life. She had become corporeal, if only for a fleeting moment before retreating into her ethereal form. We never made contact again. And then she was just gone.

Later that semester I was on the checkout line for lunch one day. "Any idea what happened to the Gray Lady?"

Her replacement was just as skinny as the Gray Lady, but much younger and masqueraded in thick eyeshadow. She handed me the change with black polished fingernails, and she smacked her gum.

"What?" She asked not looking up.

"Nothing," I said.

I thought about her again that morning as I walked past the cafeteria. Most of the school was lively at that time in the morning, so I wasn't prepared for the cold, or dark, or even the solitude of the chapel. It was empty and silent before the late morning mass. The thud of a bible hitting a bench, awakened me. Like an impending dusk, the enormous shadow of Brother Big rose above the pews. He motioned me with one finger to join him.

He moved his size with complete silence, and often a wayward student would find himself surprised to be unexpectedly face to face with Brother Big's small eyes behind the glasses, and his crop of curled and receding salty hair. I threw off my jacket, grabbed a pile of the bibles, and began to place them in the pews.

"You are late," he said.

"I'm sorry Brother. It wasn't intentional."

"'How long will you lie down, O sluggard? When will you arise from your sleep?'" he said.

I wasn't sure how to respond to that one. He saw my confusion, and when I didn't answer, he continued. "It's a common thread with the seniors. What you fail to realize is that you are responsible for your actions." He stopped midway with one bible in his hand. "None of you really seem to understand that." He opened the bible and pointed to the verse in proverbs.

"It *is* raining," I said finally, but there was no answer.

I had started placing the bibles in the side rows of the chapel. Brother Big wore the traditional black robe of the Christian Brothers, which made him more ominous, a great moving mass of black that came in and out of the shadows. Up close I noticed that the vestments under his chin were unbuttoned and that he wore a plain white t-shirt. Above the neck of the t-shirt sprouts of grayish hair, the same as the top of his head, poked out and curled. A bit of sweat was beading on his forehead. He sneezed once, pulled out a handkerchief, and rubbed furiously at his already chafed and red nose. It was only then that I noticed he had a bit of a cold.

"You are graduating at the top of your class."

"Thank you, Brother."

At that, he stared at me above his glasses. "Perhaps you have considered graduating at the top of Ridgefield's senior class instead.

With your dossier you may even still claim that scholarship to The Massachusetts Institute of Technology, even with the black mark of an expulsion."

Ridgefield was the town that I lived in, and without my scholarship to Seton Prep, Ridgefield high school would have been my home.

"I don't follow."

"Cut the *bull-shit*," he said, slamming shut the bible that he was holding. His expletive echoed off the domed ceiling and hung in the air of the chapel. "Have you applied yet to Ridgefield High School?"

"No, Brother."

"Then I suggest you do that. Since that is where you clearly intend to reside."

He rearranged the bibles and began inserting place holders to mark the hymns that we would sing at mass later.

"You intentionally left early on Monday at one-fifteen after fifth period, twice on Wednesday of last week at one-ten, fifth period," he said. "That is intention. Deliberate. Knowing."

The school had exactly one hundred and ninety-seven students in the senior graduating class. In his insane attention to detail, Brother Big could pinpoint just about every senior's grade point average, and apparently every move that you made. One hundred and ninety-seven of us. Beneath the narrow, faulty eyes, and his quiet demeanor was a deep well of contextual awareness for adolescent behavior. His questions were never arbitrary. He would ask a student, "How is your uncle's gout?" "Why did you score, beneath your ability on that Calculus exam?"

He truly did not miss even an ant crawling up the wall. I did skip study hall several times now. I had successfully aced every class that The Prep had to offer.

"Do you understand the punishment for skipping class?"

"No Brother."

"'The Lord detests lying lips.'"

I heard the distant first bell for homeroom. We both turned toward the hall that led to the school.

"Never mind that" he said. "Who started the altercation between you and Anderson?" Brother Big said. "From what I understand none of this was intentional. Was it?"

He was wrong on that one. Chaz Anderson was the bona fide all-star of Seton Prep jackasses. Chaz Anderson had facial hair the first semester of freshman year. He had arms the size of legs, and legs the size of tree trunks. Chaz starred on the football team, of course. Chaz was going to Yale. He was a moron. His family name was etched in just about every keystone of every new building at the Prep. I didn't like Chaz. I had had enough of him.

"He claims you took a swing at him," he said.

"I did."

"Pretty brave," he said. "A sloppy right cross as I see it."

Although I didn't really like Chaz, I had no reason to fight him. I was essentially invisible to him and the rest of the Prep. I was a pariah to some because I had busted the curve on most of the school tests. But that was the extent of my reputation with him and the rest of the school. A ghost. I had never been in a fist fight before.

"Dodged by a much larger, more fit, more athletic Anderson, who then responded with an overhand right of his own," Brother Big said.

I think that he had planned to hold his gaze for long enough to break me, but another violent sneeze rattled him. I imagined that he wanted some form of an explanation. Perhaps, he had misinterpreted the entire event, and now he would have to deal with Chaz as well.

"I really don't mind about Anderson," he said.

I put down the Bibles and circled around the pew. "He's an asshole," I said.

I rearranged the bibles on the pew so that the hymn books would sit on top. When I looked up, Brother Big was inches from my face, close enough to smell the incense that had burrowed into his clothes.

"'Give to Caesar what is Caesar's!'" he bellowed.

He sat down and folded his hands on the bible. "You're graduating at the top of your class in a very difficult curriculum," he said. "Sometimes it's not the earthquake that kills someone. It's the aftershocks."

"It's pleasant to speak in metaphors," I said.

He ignored my idiotic comment. He looked toward the stained-glass windows. Christ was falling for a third time and being whipped by Roman soldiers.

"You have to understand something. It's not to say that I'm not impressed by you. I am. I'm astounded by what you went through and still stayed the course," he said.

He took off his glasses, pulled a Kleenex from somewhere inside his robes and shined the lenses. He folded his enormous arms onto his chest and stared at me.

"That Sex Pistols shirt that you are wearing beneath your uniform constitutes – to you - a flagrant act of defiance. That defiance being a full-throated, spit-hurling scream in the face of a stoic and ill-conceived devotion to order that is, at best, outdated, and at worst, tied to a hypocritically old adage that is, in your estimate, to ultimately turn the other cheek."

He again cleaned his already clean glasses. How could he possibly know that I wore a Sex Pistols shirt underneath my uniform?

"Mr. Camden. Turn the other cheek and you get a razor through it.'" He bowed his head and smirked. I was missing the joke. "Who among us is the true 'an-ar-CHIST,' Mr. Camden? Is it the agitator for agitation's sake, the individualistic thrust to the parry of the faceless machine? Or, is it the rule follower who truly rebels?" He wiped his glasses again. "'No temptation has overtaken you that is not common to man.' Corinthians."

"Brother?"

"Your dissatisfaction is nothing new, Brogan. It is the curse of the thinking man. You are such a man, Mr. Camden, which is why your recent spate of impulsivity is so disappointing. Perhaps, a Che Guevara shirt would have been more suited."

He paused once more. "I can see even now that you aren't listening."

"I'm just trying to follow."

"My father was an alcoholic also," he said.

Will, my father, was now three years sober.

He leaned toward me. The gray curly hairs. The sickness on his breath.

"In short, Mr. Camden. You need more vigilance now more than ever. Proverbs 16:18 – 'Pride goes before destruction, and a haughty spirit before a fall.'"

He stopped and stared down at his hands.

I didn't speak.

"That path of the prideful and the path of the haughty spirit is a slippery slope, Brogan. I commend you on your efforts here. I admire your brilliance. But, it's not my chief concern. The pathway to the pure soul is to preserve the intellect, the comportment."

He stood to his full height and the Christ on the cross was above his head. I didn't look away. I was the number one academic student for four years straight. No one even knew who the hell I was. I was annoyed that he was putting me on par with the Chaz Andersons, with the faceless and mindless drift of Seton Prep.

"Let's pray," he said. He forcibly pushed me onto the knee stool. He made the sign of the cross, looked up to make sure that I was following suit, and then bowed his head. He was quiet for so long that I thought that he had fallen asleep.

I pretended to pray my own silent prayer. When we said "Amen," he grabbed me by the lapels of my jacket and dragged me through the pew, up the aisle, and then back behind the stage/altar. The golden box of the aumbry sat in the corner with two candles on each side. I had never been back here before. He plopped me into a chair and I waited while he fixed his robes.

He turned back to my reflection.

The Massachusetts Institute of Technology in Boston had sent me an early acceptance letter. M.I.T.. Everyone was having a baby over that one. Will and Linda could not have been prouder. Brother Big was beside himself. Father James, our school principal, called me into his office at least once a week to warn me of the dangers of straying from the path. He told me not to worry about the girls and the partying and the troublemakers, and complacency, and the lure of marijuana, and blah, blah, blah. Sure, Chaz Anderson was going to Yale because of his moronic legacy. I was a different story. I was a dark horse.

"I think that it is time you said something in your defense."

"I have no defense." What could I say? More importantly, what did he want me to say? "Timelines are beginning to write themselves, a charted course of college, career, marriage, children, old age, and the inevitable death, a Fibonacci sequence, building one upon the next, an exponential and compounding fate that really I don't have much interest in pursuing," I said.

He stopped fixing his robes and turned around. "That's very poetic, Mr. Camden. I'm not impressed."

He was the one quoting proverbs.

"You were friends with Daniel Wundt," he said.

"Yeah, Dan. The one that is now in the ground," I said. "Yes, I was."

He grabbed by my Seton Prep jacket again with one hand and dragged me out from the back room and into the private quarters of the brothers' residence. This secreted world was all new territory. Father Mulcahy was seated at an alcove in the kitchen, reading a newspaper and eating a donut like a normal human being. He looked up once, and then went back to his breakfast. Brother Big left and then returned with a few manila envelopes. He plopped down in a chair next to me.

Dan had been my best friend since I was thirteen. He taught me about sex. Graffiti. How to buy liquor by standing in front of the liquor store and paying someone to buy us a six pack of beer.

Brother Big flipped through the file. "Suicide," he said.

I see Dan Wundt sliding down the hill, a half-spent cigarette in his mouth, denim-jacketed, dark sunglasses and his head knocking to a Sony Walkman. I see him on the Schwinn wildly riding down my hill, jumping from the bike, and leaving it unmanned to crash into the fence. Dan fishing another stolen cigarette from his inner jacket. His hip hilted with spray paint cans. His fingernails blotted in blood ink, shoulders slumped, a stuttered walk with a rhythmic saunter of coolness. A backpack slung over his shoulder, stuffed with Playboy magazines and clacking with pirated cassette tapes. Dan, tackling me and making me smell his fingers, after he just stuck them into Meredith Carlson. Dan giving me a Sex Pistols t-shirt. Dan, now in the dirt at Washington cemetery, sandwiched between Mildred Holmes, and Walter Houseman.

"That's the rumor," I said.

He took his glasses off and rubbed the bridge of his nose. He was trying not to sneeze again. His eyes were watery from the cold.

"The rumor," he repeated more to himself. He breathed a heavy sigh and stared straight ahead. "Have you spoken to anyone about this?" he asked.

I didn't answer.

When I found him, one arm was duct-taped to Dan's ankle before he did it. A cigarette dangling from his mouth. He knew that if he taped his arm to his leg that there was no turning back.

"Is that what all this sudden departure is about? Do you want to speak to anyone about this?"

A great mess of piss and shit ran down to Dan's dangling combat-booted foot.

I didn't answer. I was afraid to look up for fear of the tears falling.

"Ok then. I'll consider the matter closed. You'll serve detention starting today, and every day after until the start of the Christmas break beginning today. If you intentionally or should I say unintentionally skip another class, be it your AP English Class or study hall, you will resume the rest of your academic career at Ridgefield High School."

"That seems excessive," I said.

"Too much of nothing can make a man ill at ease. One man's temper might rise while another man's temper might freeze. In the day of confession, we cannot mock a soul. When there's too much of nothing, no one has control."

"Psalms?"

"Bob Dylan."

THE FORECAST SAID something about a possible snow-storm. The house creaked its old bones and somewhere the clock clicked off the seconds.

I thought about calling my somewhat, ex-girlfriend, Andrea a half a dozen times since I had seen her at a school dance on Halloween. I had really been a winner at that one. Truly invisible. I dressed as the spaceman from the MTV commercials. Andrea said I was a "Space Oddity." She actually wrote the name in lipstick on the front of my helmet.

The long holiday weekend was wide open. The Seton Prep football game was on Saturday, but I was certain to sit that one out. I had Andrea's number on an old cafeteria napkin. She had given it to me at the dance before she left. Maybe we could get a cup of coffee. Catch up. Make out (she had actually taught me the French kiss when I was in fourth grade). We had dated for a time when I was a sophomore. That is until the prick, Rich Laforte, stole her from me. Rich Laforte was the reigning heavyweight champ of our town in a town where everyone was always knocking the snot out of one another for one reason or another. He was the Chaz Anderson of Ridgefield with a lot less money, a lot more looks, and an incomparable amount of toughness.

I picked up the phone and put it down a few times. I was sweat-ing like an idiot, and it was freezing in the house. My heart was bopping a Neil Peart drum solo. I dialed the number. The phone rang a few times, and then I noticed the clock. It was 5:30 a.m. I hung up.

In the quiet of my misery, I recognized the sound of coffee being brewed. Will was up early. I just keep sitting there and wondering why I couldn't be smooth, like Dan was. He had taught me enough.

The phone rang. I imagined it was her calling back, and about to give me a royal ration of shit for waking her up at 5:30. I nearly broke my leg trying to bet back to the phone in time. I grabbed the line and whispered a "hello," but I was too late. A conversation had already begun. It was not Andrea.

In the pause, I coughed.

"Brogan, hang up the phone…now," Will said on the other line.

I cradled the phone and shortly after I heard Will walk down the stairs and head directly to the basement. The first drifts of cigarette smoke filtered up through the door. I followed soon afterwards and waited in the kitchen. It wasn't long before I heard Linda descending the stairs and then joining Will in the basement. I listened by the door.

Linda's voice came in harsh whispers. Since Will stopped drinking, he rarely raised his voice. It seemed as though that life was one that died four years ago when he had given it up for good. Now, to hear that demon resurrected, and the harsh chords of anger coming from the basement, was not good.

"Boy!" Will called from the basement.

Boy. That was his new name for me. Linda was steaming mad about something, and I was sure that I was on the chopping block for this one. I was certain it was Brother Big. I had no intention of serving that detention the day before. Even if it meant a stint at Ridgefield High. We had wrapped up the day with an early mass in the freezing chapel on Tuesday and then I parted hastily from the Christian Brothers for the long weekend. As our bus pulled away I could see Brother Big in front of the school, his great being, holding a clipboard, looking in the distance, and then calmly returning to the school.

Will was sitting in his favorite chair next to a cluttered desk with an overfilled ashtray. The smoke from his cigarette squinted one of his eyes.

"Who was on the phone, Will?" I ask.

"You know, smartass. I remember a time and place when you called me Dad or Pop."

"Who was on the phone, Pop?"

WILL STOOD IN the mugged light of a late autumn day with his half-lit cigarette, jeans, white t-shirt, and work boots. The gutters had been cleaned. The lawn was aerated and patterned in rows. The azaleas had been wrapped. The dogwoods could sleep for another season. We worked in silence. He put away the leaf-blower, the rakes, the broom. I collected the piled leaves into bags and set them by the curb.

"So - Uncle Frank is coming to Thanksgiving?"

He stopped raking. "That's not exactly the situation," Will said.

"What is the situation?"

"Well, he is coming."

Tomorrow, the family would be coming for Thanksgiving dinner. Linda was an octopus in the kitchen, arms flailing from burner to burner, with the wrenching sound of the opening and closing oven, and the whirring torrent of mixers working simultaneously. She was a one-person show.

Will and Linda started hosting Thanksgiving dinner when Will became sober. The first year was enough to make Will almost go back to the sauce, and for Linda to almost jump out the window by the end of the night. She wasn't prepared for the hoopla of a family Thanksgiving dinner. Nor was she ready for Uncle George to just about drop dead when he learned that booze was off limits. (Aunt Margaret directed him to return the bottle of Jack Daniels to the car.

He disappeared for a few pulls throughout the day). Everyone found Linda to be quite the host, not to mention her great casserole, and from then on, Beechwood Avenue became the hub of Thanksgiving, and Christmas, and Easter, President's Day, Arbor Day, and any other day where she could cook herself silly.

In less than twenty-four hours the fanfare would begin, uncles hollering over the usefulness of labor unions, the price of Lucky Strikes, the New York Yankees bullpen, who was the best fighter of all time, Ali, Frazier, Mike Tyson. The asthmatic radiators wheezed steam. The late fall sunlight slanted on overloaded parlor tables of meat gravy, whipped yams, yards of kielbasa, creamed corn, and jellied deserts. With the wheezed out slanted holiday, the totes of swollen tin-foiled trays of turkey, the Manicotti and the red wine, the coffee, our collection of copper-plated, pickled aunts and uncles, the screaming litters of newborn cousins (they doubled in population with every holiday, I swear), and a dog barking somewhere, Beechwood Avenue became a three-ring circus that was just shy of sending Linda to Bellevue for a much needed convalescent weekend, equipped with one of those jackets that she could hug herself in all day long, with all the applesauce she could eat.

And now, she had Uncle Frank to add to the mix

The floor moaned beneath the uneasy romping of Linda upstairs. Closet doors were opened and slammed. The bed creaked. Her footsteps made an uneven pace in the bedrooms above, and with a sharp snap, sheets that had been cleaned and replaced just the day before were whipped into heaps on the floor and laundered again. The whishing of a mop came next, followed by the scrubbing of the shower and toilet. Linda was tempered glass, transparent and fluid in a life of sustained rituals and stability, able to absorb the bullet of disruption, but shattered nonetheless, and restrained in a web of cracks. Passing Linda and Will's bedroom that morning, I found that she still had not corrected her student essays.

She liked to swear in private. After the laundry was settled and the floors dampened and the shower primed for the third time in two days, she let out a long, furious "Fucking Frank!"

Not since Will was away at the Sunrise Rehabilitation house had she spoken to the painting of Jesus on the wall, and now she was in a full conversation. "Why now? Give me patience, Lord. Please, don't let me murder every goddamn one of them."

"Snowflakes! That is what Frank calls women!" Linda said to Will in her hushed but aggressive voice. I heard Will chuckle a bit. "It's not funny." Linda said and then mimicked a man's voice. "'They fall in their white beauty.' Yeah, he told me that at your cousin's wedding while they were walking her down the aisle. 'Sometimes they are soft, or they are compact and hard.' Then he leans in and tells me 'Sometimes they are even dirty!' Really William. I can't handle this today. Not now. Not today!"

"He's a man of appetites," Will said.

"So, he says! And don't be cute with me, Will. This is not a time to be funny. If I remember correctly, he was the one that started a fight at the same wedding by humping one of the married bridesmaids in the walk-in cooler Yes, Will. Remember that graceful move?"

Uncle Frank was coming? The Phantom. That would be a daisy.

WILL STARTED THE car and waited in the driveway. He needed a break from Linda. Sometimes, without an audience, she wasn't as vocal, and she would take a break from shouting to sneak a cigarette.

I always took the ride with Will the day before the holiday, and we picked up the last of the Italian meats and the Kielbasa for Thanksgiving dinner. When he used to drink, he would take the opportunity to get out of the house, and we would stop at the Jade East Chinese restaurant where he would drink several Mai Tai's, any one of which could put a mere mortal on Jupiter. Now, we just followed tradition, minus the Mai Tai's. He was silent for the ride and listened to his jazz.

I know that Will would not do this intentionally, but we passed by Washington Cemetery. Beneath the white coating of snow, and the hard frozen ground, the remains of my friend were rotting away.

"Did you want to stop?" Will asked.

I shook my head no.

Dipalma's deli had been a stop for as long as I could remember, a squat cement building more toward the industrial side of town. Will was lost in thought and drove through a light drift of an early snowfall. By the time we reached the store it was just past ten, Dipalma himself was outside throwing salt on the sidewalk. For years he and Will would smoke cigarettes in the back. Dipalma was a great mass of an Italian with thick sideburns, and he wore a smock blood-stained from the butchering that he did on his own in the back of the store. Will still brought him a bottle of Johnny Walker Black for the holiday. Will drank an espresso at a metal table, and Dipalma drank the scotch. They gave a "cheers" and then complained about the New York Giants and the local politicians, their wives, and just about anything to chew on while they smoked a few more cigarettes. A customer came in and Dipalma disappeared to the front.

Will waited until Dipalma was out of earshot.

"Your mother is upset."

"Do you think?" I asked sarcastically. "What's going on?"

"Never mind," he said. "You know that we are very proud of you."

In the low light of the storeroom, I could see a mountain of pain weighing on his mind.

"With that being said, your mother says that you are second guessing everything."

"I have that right."

"Some nonsense about Europe or Los Angeles or some horseshit like that."

"It's a thought."

Back in his drinking days, Will had taken me to the annual County Police softball game. At Corky's bar and grill, the cops' local watering hole, I saw Will fight for the first time. I was eleven. The altercation began with a few joking words between Will and a bearded man that everyone claimed was a Judo expert. A switch had been thrown with Will when the man crossed into dangerous territory, which was saying something about my mother, Will's wife. Within seconds, Will had the man between the barstools and was punching at his throat, not trying to simply win the fight, but I imagine to end his life. The swift change in his nature from joking to manic violence was a testament to a hair trigger temper, more pronounced after several Jameson's Irish Whisky, but now, even in sobriety, still present, and to be approached as warily as a mountain lion. Although his anger had never been delivered to me with the same intensity of intention, I usually remained cautious.

"Are you out of your fucking mind?" Will asked.

Yes, I did feel like that at times. I didn't answer. Will was getting into a lather, and I really couldn't blame him. He never had the opportunity to go to college. He began to chew on the bottom of his mustache, a sure indication that his temperature gauge was skyrocketing perilously into the red. I wasn't planning on acting on any of Dan's misadventures, but the thought was still there, like that noisy cricket in the room that you can't find. I wanted to tell Will, but now was not the time. He was acting strange. And dangerous. It was time for me to shut up.

"You know Frank is a lot of trouble," he said more to himself, draining the last of his espresso. "He reminds me of half of the people that I locked up."

What did I care if he was trouble or not. He wrote weird letters. And everyone had a funny story about him.

Just then, Dipalma returned from the front. We would continue the conversation another time.

Uncle Frank was trouble. Trouble felt good.

Happy Birthday Brogan

Angels and demons will come to your doorstep. Just be aware of which is which. Sometimes they are the same. Don't give in to the money game. It is sooner than you think that you will be worm food. Be tough. Some days it's elephants, some days it's peanuts. Stay in shape, chase girls, and dance. For Chrissakes, don't forget to do the dance.

Love, Frank.

WE RETURNED TO the house an hour later. A gleaming bullet of a Chevy Nova was parked in the driveway. Will shook his head. He sat in the car, listened to more of his jazz cassette tapes, and just stared out of the window. The house was an unexploded grenade. With the pin already pulled. We grabbed the groceries from the trunk and walked inside.

When Linda returned to the house four years ago, she had a thing about smoking inside. Will could have his cigars and cigarettes in the basement only. I smelled the acrid smoke as soon as I entered. Linda was seated at the kitchen table with her own cigarette. Her arms were folded, and her legs were crossed. I hadn't seen her smoke openly since I was younger. She defiantly blew the smoke toward us. She looked like she was about to "spit nails," one of her favorite expressions for when she was really pissed off.

"Welcome back, boys," she said.

Seated on the other side of the table was a man that I guessed to be in his late forties or early fifties. He was bald, with a big handlebar mustache. I wondered how he can eat through that mustache. Just above the neckline of his shirt, I could see a cheap looking tattoo on his neck. A set of two playing cars, a joker and an ace of spades.

"Well, here he is," Linda said. "Sure as shit and in the living flesh."

Now I could really tell that Linda was in a huff. It was the second time that I had heard her curse that day.

"Hello, Will," the man said. He stood, intending to give Will a hug but Will grew rigid, so he settled for a handshake. When he stood, the gasoline smell made me think that the air would explode at any moment. It was a familiar smell. Will shook hands. He set the groceries down and leaned against the counter.

The man looked down on me. He was taller, about six foot one and broad chested.

"Well, Frank," Will finally said, exasperated. "This is Brogan. Brogan, this is your uncle. Frank."

Linda stubbed out the cigarette, stood up, and went to the living room. A service door separated the living room from the kitchen and was usually propped open. Linda kicked aside the door jamb and the door swung shut. Linda was pissed.

"Uncle Frank?" I asked.

"Just Frank is OK," he said.

Even a few feet away Frank was about as near as a constellation. He was one of those construed images of the ancients, putting all those dots together in the sky to form an image of a god. That god of thieves, I thought. Mercury, the one with winged sandals that Mrs. Murray had taught us about in mythology class.

To hear Aunt Margaret or Uncle George, or Linda, or my own father, Frank was nothing more than that phantom, perhaps a demon from the few snippets of conversation that I was able to hear at our family gatherings. Philanderer, con artist, gambler.

So, this was the mystery man from the letters. He looked like an overworked mechanic by the way that he dressed. His face was weathered but handsome, with sharp, blue eyes. Baldness doesn't fit most men, but for Frank, it was perfect. He wore a black and white flannel shirt, blue jeans, and black engineer boots. He held his sunglasses in his hand. Frank was not a part of the family photos that Will kept in a shoebox. He looked nothing like I imagined.

Frank picked up his own pack of cigarettes off the table and offered one to Will. I heard Linda in the other room. "Will!"

Will left us alone in the room and joined Linda in the living room.

I took a seat at the table. "Uncle Frank?"

"I said that just Frank is ok. If that's not too much of a stretch for you."

"OK, Frank. Where do you live now?"

Frank looked either amused or bored. I wasn't sure.

"Here and there. Mostly there, where it's not so cold."

"Where is that?"

Frank looked at me and smirked. "Where it's warm."

I had to smile.

The radiator hissed its hacked, wheezed breath and banged a protest. The flooring in the kitchen was a heavy orange linoleum tile with a checkered pattern that, if you stared at it too long, it became three-dimensional and formed tumbling squares. I summoned the ghosts of the past and tried to will my aunts and uncles into the room to break the tension. Frank paced in the kitchen, appearing whole and then falling into patterns, like the floor. It was hard to imagine that he was actually flesh and blood, and not just the scattered messages of eighteen years from those tinted envelopes, half-stories, and nonsensical letters, and wallpaper checks.

When my parents' voices breached a whisper in the living room, Frank suddenly pulled a short, red instrument from his pocket. It was a kazoo. He began to play and he was actually not too bad. He stood up and did a funny dance around the kitchen table. The odd instrument twanged, spitting offbeat notes from the kitchen wall almost like a voice, giving that phantom his own language. Then a tune began to emerge. It sounded a bit like *Jumping Jack Flash*. He looked like a lunatic. But he was funny, and he probably knew that the kazoo was annoying the hell out of my father. Then just as suddenly, he stopped and stuffed the kazoo back into his chest pocket.

"What do you want to drink?" he said, growing restless and opening and closing the refrigerator door. "Beer, juice, a Coke? Did I say a beer?" The mustache rumbled above his mouth.

"It's eleven o'clock in the morning."

"So, what do you want to drink?"

"A beer."

He pulled two old, mismatched glasses from the pantry and grabbed a can of beer from the refrigerator. It was only in the last year, due largely to a protest from Uncle George, that Linda allowed booze back in the house on a holiday. She was ever vigilant about it and kept a strict inventory on every consumed drop.

Frank poured half of a beer into each of our glasses, winked, and raised a toast. "Tits and tonsils, he said. He paused for a long space and eyed me with a crooked smile. I had no idea what "tits and tonsils" meant, but I raised my glass anyway.

"You're a beer man," Frank said.

"Excuse me?"

He drained the glass in one long gulp and then reached for another beer.

"A man's drink defines him."

A beer man was reassuring. Just to be called any kind of man one time.

"Two things! Never let anyone photograph you without a drink. Remember this. It's important. Secondly, never trust a person who doesn't drink."

"I never saw you in any photographs."

"No shit," he said.

"My father doesn't drink."

Frank laughed. "I know. Trust me. He just doesn't drink anymore."

"Are you a beer man?" I asked.

"Bourbon."

"How do you know which one you are?"

"It depends on your personality." He opened and closed the cabinets until he found the liquor. "Your old man sure has a lot of booze for someone off the sauce."

I wanted to hear his assessment of what constituted a beer man versus a bourbon man. I want to pin his theory down philosophically, what relation it had to Plato's forms, whether this holy endowment was changeless and eternal. Was there an undiscovered algorithm to determine through immutable, mathematical means whether and why you are a "beer man?" Or was it astrology, like a horoscope, and the way that you want to believe in some mystical power of the alignment of the stars and the movement of the galaxies, and the way every horoscope is kind of universal, but you twist it to be intimate to you, and say to yourself, "oh my god, that's me," but somehow knowing in your soul it's all just bullshit. But you kind of want to believe it anyway.

He looked over the stock of alcohol in the cabinet, removing bottles, measuring the contents in his mind, and then replacing them.

"It's for the holidays. How do you know that I'm a beer man?" I asked.

"How do you know a triangle is a perfect triangle?"

"Because it has three equal sides?"

"You are right, but how does that make it perfect? Remember this, there are always three sides to every story. That's another important lesson for another time. And, in the same way, this is just as mathematical. You see, vodka drinkers are on a slide to dementia. It's simply an anesthetic tonic, clear and tasteless. That just doesn't seem like you. Not as far as I can tell. But we will see. Vodka is like sedation. Think about it. Do you want to be something that can mix with everything? You have too much character for that. And sense. Christ! Have you ever seen a normal Russian? Rum drinkers are cursed. Too many umbrellas and sugar. Sugar is no good for a fit man. Too many crazy Jamaicans with rum. And gin! Forget about gin right now! It's for the criminally insane. Don't play games with me on this. It's those goddamn juniper berries." He paused now and looked at me closely. "But beer, beer is a working man's boost, a shot in the arm of a scrapper."

"That is in no way mathematical," I said. I knew mathematics. Better than most college seniors.

"Oh, but it is," Frank said. "You're a scrapper."

I felt honored.

"You just don't know it yet."

I felt deflated.

He removed a bottle of bourbon from the cabinet where Linda kept all the booze in the house and from where she could carefully monitor the contents.

"But bourbon, it's the voice of the poets and the aristocracy," he said and poured himself a shot. He held that bottle up and raised his eyebrows as if he were offering me a drink. I shook my head no.

"What about wine?"

"That's for women."

"I want to be a bourbon guy, then."

"That's an earned position."

He studied me again without speaking and sipped on his beer. I felt the mild buzz of the beer settling in.

"Now that we are two men having a drink, I want to know something."

"Okay."

"Do you have a girlfriend?"

"No."

"Do you have several girlfriends?"

"No."

"Is there something wrong with you?"

"Like what?"

"Well, you're a goddamn good-looking, young guy. I figure you should be chasing girls from the minute you wake up with a hard-on."

Frank wanted answers.

"School keeps me busy."

He laughed while raising his beer, all the while staring me right in the eyes. I tried to look away, but he followed my gaze, forcing me to look at him straight.

"What?"

"There is nothing more important than that sacred place that you'll find between their legs. Keep busy at that," he said.

WILL AND LINDA were in the doorway of the kitchen. "And now, my son is goddamned drinking," Linda said. Will diffused the situation by dumping the last of my glass of beer down the drain and then gathered us back into the living room. We sat in a circle like a therapy session, Linda's foot tapped at an accelerated rate, and Frank sat perfectly still with his hands folded on his lap.

"This is no bullshit, Frank," Will said.

"What is your point, Will?"

"This is real life. These are real live people you are talking to," Will said.

"Oh, for Christ's sake," Frank said. "What is that supposed to mean?"

"You and reality are not often on speaking terms. That is what I mean. It means you're not just sending a letter and a check and that there are consequences. Why this? Why now?" Will asked. "We are not taking any chances on him. He's going to college. Did you know that?"

"I think we all know the answer to that, Will. Don't worry. I'll bring him back in one piece," he said.

"Your Uncle Frank would like you to accompany him for the weekend, Brogan," Linda said to me.

"I have school on Monday."

"There we have it," Linda said.

"You are off *until* Monday though," Frank said very slowly and very matter of fact.

Will looked at the ground trying to avoid the intense stare and mounting tension of Linda.

As much as I admired Frank, my admiration for him was like that for a movie villain, fun to watch on the screen, but something to be safely regarded from a distance. I didn't even really know who the hell he was. He had the fascination of a historical figure. Someone that I wouldn't mind meeting, but certainly wouldn't want to spend a weekend camping with. I begged my father with my eyes to make the decision for me and say "no," but that privilege sailed when I made other decisions: to drive, to go to college, or even to have a beer. Resolutions volleyed between certainty and uncertainty: a labyrinth of potential wrong turns.

"What about Thanksgiving?" I asked.

"There will be plenty of turkey," Frank said.

"Where would we be going?"

Frank stared directly at me. "Everywhere."

"I can't!" Linda screamed. "Are you kidding me? You are going to let a junked-out loser, a scammer, a criminal take off with our only child. I can't believe that this is even a discussion. In fact, case closed. Brogan, get upstairs to your room, and you," she said, pointing to Frank, "hit the bricks."

"I'm not going to my room," I said.

"Linda let's take a minute to consider the situation," Will said. He began to chew on his mustache.

"I don't need a minute. You sit here and you coddle him, and you act like everything is fine. The only thing that confuses me, is why all of you find it necessary to kowtow to this lunatic. The whole family! Every one of you!"

"It's not about that. Brogan needs to make his own decision on this one."

"Who? Brogan? Every decision that we have made until now has led him to where he is, and it's turned out pretty damn good. Look at him. Your son is going to M.I.T.," she said very slowly. "Unheard of. He has a chance. A good chance at this life. The reason being we have kept him from ending up on the floor with people like Frank."

Frank just continued to look at me and smile.

"I don't kowtow to anyone," Will said, coming unhinged. "This is family. This is my brother, his uncle."

"Well, good! Fine, then! Come on over tomorrow! Pull up a chair and have a drink, Frank. We're going to do something that may seem extraordinary and wildly unfamiliar to you—we are going to have dinner with a turkey and mashed potatoes on Thanksgiving with significant people in our life."

"That's why I'm here," Frank said.

"He wants to get to know him," Will said. "He does have that right."

"Well, let's see what Brogan knows so far," Linda said. "Frank drinks beer at eleven o'clock in the morning and shares it with underage children. He encourages irresponsible sexual behavior. He writes unintelligible, caustic notes to him on his birthday, accompanied by bad checks, and then shows up the day before the holiday, our holiday, our time, and wants to take him away. That's exactly the type of person that I want to have chaperone my child. Maybe Ted Bundy will show up next, and they can have a round of badminton. Not happening. Not in this life."

Linda was up and pacing the room. She stopped, collected her thoughts, and breathed deeply. Frank remained silent.

"I tolerate you at the very least, Frank. Because I must. You are William's brother. But you are dangerous. I don't have to let you do this, no matter what you think is your right. I don't want you to see Brogan. I don't want you to know him, not like this. You are an interruption. I have papers to grade next week, a dinner to cook for thirty people. Brogan has his schoolwork to think of. He has worked very hard to get here, and we have protected that effort. We can't let anything get in the way. If you want to stay for dinner, you are welcome, but that is the extent of it."

Frank continued to look only at me.

"What do you think?" Frank asked.

"I've already told you what I think," Linda said.

"I wasn't talking to you."

"It doesn't matter what he thinks," Will said.

"I thought that you said it does," Frank said.

"I don't know what I think," I said.

"Well, that is a position that you rarely want to find yourself in. Perhaps he could use some of my tutelage."

My father began to gnaw heavily on his mustache.

Linda locked onto Will, and then stood and exited the room in a rage of disgust. Although she was tiny, she could hold an entire room. Her absence left a hollow silence. She had made her case, but as strong as it was, Will was the ultimate judge and jury.

Linda was in the kitchen now, distracting herself with the creamed corn and stuffing the manicotti. Will and Frank left to smoke on the porch and, from the look of it, to have a private conversation. I joined Linda and watched them from the window.

The conversation got heated at times. The air was gasoline once again, as if it could fuel them, or suddenly ignite and blow up the whole situation.

"I wonder what they are arguing about."

"I know Frank seems fun and mysterious, you have heard all of the stories before, and everyone laughs at his antics, and that is fine, but it's not fine for you. There's a lot that you don't know. You *are* old enough to make your own decisions, but with this, I have to draw the line."

"That is a pretty cool car," I said, looking at Frank's Chevy Nova.

33

"Are you listening to me?"

"I understand," I said.

"Besides, you have the Thanksgiving Day football game, and don't you want to spend that with your friends before you are off to school?"

"I don't have any friends."

She ignored the last comment. The phone rang again, and soon Linda was explaining to her sister that my father's "nutcase brother just showed up."

"No, I couldn't imagine him staying for dinner, and most definitely no, he is certainly not taking Brogan, even if Jesus himself were riding shotgun. No, that is not blasphemy. It's the goddamn truth." More curses.

"God, that is a cool fucking car," I said.

"Brogan, don't use that word," Linda admonished, pinching the phone between her shoulder and ear.

"But you did," I said.

I FOUND THAT SAME Sex Pistols t-shirt beneath a pile of old corduroy pants and V-neck Seton Prep sweater. I slipped on the wrinkled shirt and looked in the mirror, a pink shirt with a splatter of the punk rock band name on the front. Dan had given me that shirt the same day that he said we were going on a road trip to Los Angeles when I graduated. He said that we were going to Paris to exhume Jim Morrison's body. He said that he wasn't going anywhere with me wearing the polo shirt and plaid shorts that I had chosen. "Not on my watch," Dan said. "Get upstairs and put this on," he said, pulling the wrinkled shirt from his backpack and throwing it at me. The shirt was skintight.

I could see Dan beneath the Main Street Bridge, the denim jacket, the spray paint cans on his hip, ready to rewrite the world. The smug and knowing look on his face. Spray-painting on the wall "We want the world, and we want it now!"

I was invisible. *Don't be pussy*, I heard Dan say.

"I want to go," I said, standing downstairs in my Sex Pistols shirt, denim jacket and boots.

Linda stopped cutting turnips and put both of her hands on the counter. She kept her back to me.

"You are not going," she said.

"Will said it's my decision."

"It's not, I'm saying it's not, and that is final."

35

She hurried the turnips, snapping off the tips and furiously chopping on the cutting board.

"You know Linda, it wasn't my choice when you cut town on Will and I."

"That is a very inaccurate and mean thing to say, Brogan. You know what I had to deal with. You know more than anyone."

Linda had still not faced me. She was motionless. I began to feel like a real shit for saying that. From the back, I could see that she was crying.

"I tried to take you with me."

"Yes, you did"

"You don't speak to your mother that way, ever." Will was behind me. When I turned around, he was chewing on his mustache. That crazy that left when the booze left him flashed for just a moment.

"I'm going," I said.

"You're not going anywhere."

"Goddammit Will, you never asked me or Mom or anyone when you left!"

"Will, don't!" Linda screamed.

You don't swear at Will. It was the first and only time that I thought Will would ever hit me. He moved forward with a clenched raised fist and checked himself before he let fly with a punch. I had never raised my voice to him. You don't raise your voice to Will. He collapsed into a chair.

"YOU GET YOUR winky wet yet?" Frank asked.

I turned to look at the head case behind the wheel.

"Excuse me?"

"Did you dip your wicket?"

I just continued to stare.

"I forgot who I was talking to. Did you make the beast with two backs?"

"Othello?"

"Are you!" He said pointing directly at me, "a fucking virgin? Jesus H. Christ!"

"Does it matter?"

"Yes."

The wind sang across the windows of Frank's supercharged Chevy Nova.

"The 1968 Chevy Nova sold more cars than any other. She's got the only year that GM offered the L79 engine. That's one hell of a heart pumping underneath there."

The countryside was a blurring landscape. Ahead of the Chevy, the road was clear, crystalline behind, but directly across, it was a marred blur of trees and houses. The seats were worn, the black vinyl smoothed, the dashboard dated, the windshield caked with road dust. Frank chain smoked, and the deeply embedded smell of tobacco was intoxicating.

"She'll go on forever, this one," Frank said patting the side of the door. "And, she had a wider wheelbase that year. So not only is she quick, but it'll take Hell to knock her over."

"That's very nice," I said. What could I say? What the hell did I know about a Chevy L79 Nova?

Frank just looked over at me with his eyes wide open with confusion. "Christ kid, you got a lot to learn."

We drove the Garden State Parkway into the country autumn of small towns. We accelerated through the leaf-blown streets and up and down the hills of northern New Jersey. The trees were ablaze in a cauldron of deep reds and orange.

"They're going to try to *make you* go to that college and all that happy horseshit," he said. "You don't have to go."

"I'm enrolled already."

"You can still quit," Frank says.

"It's a great school."

"Big deal."

"They deny ninety-seven percent of their applicants."

"Oh my."

"I got a scholarship."

"Whoopdie fucking doo."

"You didn't go to college."

"How do you know?"

I didn't know.

"It was just a different sort of college," he said.

"Anyway, I think that I want to go."

"You think?"

"I really don't know."

He stubbed another cigarette butt into the overgrown forest of an ashtray and sighed. He sped up as we crossed into the next town.

"It's all vigorish," Frank said. "You see, you can place your bet now, and stack up the odds in your favor. College, a degree, a good job. But remember this: if you take the safe bet and lose, life is going to smack you in the ass with a pretty hefty vig."

"What's a vig?" I asked.

"It's the juice. It's the butter. It's the extra price you pay when you are wrong."

Frank had this idea of picking apples and bringing them to Linda. He thought that she would want to make apple pies for Thanksgiving. I think he saw it as some kind of peace pipe, or just a way to fit in. I was positive that Linda couldn't care less about making pies and would probably scream at the thought of another task. She had her hands full enough with the turkey and a seven-course meal that an army couldn't finish, not to mention a pile of mid-term papers she needed to correct after everyone had left. And not to mention, her only son was off with a loose cannon. But maybe Frank wasn't that stupid. When he downgraded his plans from weekend jaunt to an afternoon of apple picking, she didn't really consent so much as she conceded, provided that "he is back in the house by sundown. I'm not joking."

It was past noon when we arrived in the small, quaint town that was already shutting down for the holiday. The parking lot for the farm was understandably vacant, except for a single car.

"They look closed," I said.

"They are closed. Grab your shit, and we'll see about that," Frank said, jumping out of the car.

A man in a stained smock was just then closing the door and he jumped at the sight of Frank.

"You get to pick your own apples here, yes?"

"Most of the time, yes, but its way past the season," he said laughing.

Frank didn't laugh.

The man in the smock stopped laughing. "We have some inside, if you want to come back, but we're locking up for the holiday."

"Already! It's only noon."

The man smiled at Frank as if he were joking. "It's now past noon. And yes. You are right. It's past noon on the day before Thanksgiving."

"Christ almighty! This guy is killing me. What if I give you a twenty?"

"Listen, pal, the place is closed for the holiday. It's a farm, not a saloon. What planet are you from anyway?"

The man walked away, and Frank spoke to himself. "He's got a point."

The storekeeper unlocked his car door, never taking his eye off Frank. When he was satisfied that we weren't a threat, he started the car. While rolling by, he waved at us. Frank dipped his head toward the window. "Planet Motherfucker, Fucko!"

The brake lights came on, and the car paused. Frank flared his arms out like a lobster. I supposed the man considered getting out but thought twice after seeing the madman in the parking lot waving his arms about.

Before we'd left the house, my father sat me down in the garage office. He handed me a hundred-dollar bill and said to keep it in case of an emergency. He said that he wasn't sure what the hell this was all about, but that I was old enough to make my own decisions.

"Frank gets the monkey on him at times. Do you know what that means?"

"Not really," I said.

"It means that he has addictions and is susceptible to bad decisions. I don't want you to be one of his bad decisions. Just watch yourself."

"I will."

"If he starts acting nuts, use that money, and grab a cab or something right away. Just get out of there. Am I clear?"

"Yes."

"Back by sundown?"

"Yes."

"If he gets in trouble, you call me. Your mother and I love you. Do you understand that?"

That was a frightening thing to hear because he had never said it before. It was his job to be a foundation of unwavering conviction. The naked revelation of his love wasn't as unnerving as his indecision.

"I'm not really sure what this is about, but just keep your head about you."

"Sure, Will." I turned to him before I left. "I'm sorry, Pop."

"No need to be sorry. This is your decision. Be tough. Just, get your ass back here on time."

He was annoyed. Frank had intruded on a ritual day that was ours and a rite that my father never shared with his own father. I think he was scared. Will didn't get scared. I guess that he was scared because I was partnered into my first Frank scheme.

I stood now in the apple-picking parking lot and wondered what was next.

"Get in the car," Frank said.

"Are we leaving?"

"Sort of."

Back in town, Frank found an open bar. He made me wait in the car while he disappeared for a moment and then returned with a bottle in a brown bag. We parked a mile down the road from the farm along the hedgerow. The Chevy was camouflaged. We locked the doors, crossed a small field, and Frank gave me a boost over the fence.

I threw one leg over the fence. "Where are we going?" I asked.

"To pick apples."

"I know. I understand that." I looked behind me. The trees were bare. "But they're closed, and it's way past apple-picking season. We should just split."

41

"I don't know. Maybe you're right. And, then again, maybe you are wrong."

"Frank, we don't even need apples. Linda's tied up enough as it is."

"Well," Frank said. "Sometimes you just can't stop a horse halfway through the water." Frank said. Whatever the hell that was supposed to mean.

In the afternoon shadows, rows of apple paths with deep wheel ruts in the mud stretched out in straight lines perpendicular to the hills. The trees were barren and clean in the harsh afternoon light. There wasn't an apple to be found, and it was cold. Apple season had ended a month ago. But Frank was determined, almost maniacal. He didn't remove his sunglasses. He told me that he was sensitive to light. "And besides," he said, sipping from the bottle, "you don't want to give up your hand."

He was a bourbon man, the so-called poet, I supposed. That's what I gathered from that little speech he had given me in the morning about booze. I was getting bored. I wanted the open road, an adventure. I guess that I wanted Frank to be something of a superhero. What I didn't want was to sit here and freeze my ass off and watch him get drunk. I had had enough nights like that in my life with Will.

Just then, Frank stood and wandered. He left the bottle and leaned against a nearby tree. This would be interesting. I kept watch on the storehouse to see if the man in the dirty smock was going to return and have us arrested for trespassing. The field and the trees were empty, and the whole thing seemed ridiculous.

I started thinking of Dan and what he would have thought of this whole fiasco. Dan would have fired up a joint, put on some headphones, and listened to The Clash. I didn't have a joint. I didn't smoke. And I didn't have a Walkman. I had some harebrained dude with an attention deficit problem.

I noticed Frank beyond a short rise in the tree-crowded meadow. He was far enough away now to be just a shadowy silhouette. He was in a runner's crouch and suddenly he made a dash across the field. And then, he repeated the same process. I was wondering if he had a football tryout somewhere that he didn't tell me about. He was thrashing against the advancing afternoon, breaking through the fields, running in fits and starts. He stopped to gather his breath, I guessed, and doubled over, and his chest heaved.

When he finally came back, he was breathing heavy. He sat down, removed his sunglasses, and studied the horizon.

"What the hell are you doing, Frank?" I asked.

"Warming up," he said.

"For what?"

He didn't have an answer to that question.

"You know there was this guy that sold the actual Eiffel Tower. Twice!"

"In Paris?"

"No. Trenton. Yes. Paris!"

"I thought the French government owned it."

"Yes. They did. You smart little son-of-a-bitch. But this guy. He fakes a bunch of government documents and convinces these contactors that they are going to tear down the tower, saying that the government can't afford the upkeep, and anyway it's more of an eyesore compared to all the other Paris monuments."

"And they believed that?"

"Let me finish," he said.

When he finally caught his breath, he pulled out his cigarettes and lit one.

"So, he gets this group together at a fancy hotel, and he singles in on this one real insecure sucka that looks like he wouldn't say boo, and who's trying to make his way up the social ladder. He convinces this guy that he is actually a corrupt government official and that this guy could bribe him for the sale. Anyway, he ends up getting a boatload of cash as a bribe, and then skips town."

"And, what?" I asked. I wasn't sure I understood the point of this story.

"And what?" he repeated. "The same cat tried the same con again, but almost got pinched."

"OK," I said.

He stomped at the cigarette "Lesson learned. Don't go to the well too often."

Frank took off his sunglasses.

"Do you get it?"

"No."

He waved a dismissive hand at me and looked around. He seemed frustrated.

"This isn't right, Frank said.

"You need to pick apples in October, not November, that's why," I said.

"No, it's not the goddamn apples. It's all of this nonsense. Turkeys and relatives and apple pies. This isn't my show, Brogan."

"I have no idea what we are doing here, Frank."

"Do you want to go home?"

"Yes. This is pointless," I said.

"Are you a gambler?" Frank asked.

"What? No. I don't know. I guess?"

"Want to race?"

"No."

"From here to the fence," he said.

The distance was a good two hundred yards. He was still gasping from his previous sprints. I wondered if he was going to need CPR. I wasn't all that excited about dragging his corpse to the car and explaining to my parents why I had killed my Uncle Frank. Besides, it didn't seem like a fair fight anyway. I was about to turn eighteen. He was, I was guessing, about fifty. He smoked, and he drank bourbon and beer for breakfast. Not exactly Olympic material. He was wearing boots.

"Hundred bucks. From here to the fence."

"Why?"

"Because I think that I can beat you."

"You have a change of shoes?"

"Fuck that."

"Frank, you almost had a heart attack earlier."

"Make a decision. I'm challenging you to a race. If you think that you can win, accept the challenge. Don't dance around the question. Make up your mind. You know, sometimes it's going to end up being a bitch of a decision. Some days it's elephants, and some days it's peanuts. Either way, you have to ante up."

"Maybe you should calm down, Frank. It really doesn't seem like that big of a deal."

"It's everything."

He stood with his hands on his hips looking into the distance, I guess waiting for an answer.

"Fine. If you put it that way, then I accept."

Upon the agreement of the bet, Frank changed into a different man. He paced, fluttering his hands and feet and loosening his core. He was focused now. Pacing. He was surprisingly flexible. But he was still out of breath.

"Frank maybe we should reconsider."

"Shut up and get ready. I intend to give you a thorough ass whoopin."

"If you say so."

Suddenly, we were not alone. It seemed that the monkey Will had mentioned was out and about. Frank was a different person.

The fury and heat were building in my bones, too. It was beginning to feel like this was a real challenge.

Frank ducked into a runner's crouch. "On three," he said.

"You mean right now?"

A part of me thought that this bet may have been a clever way to give me a present of a hundred bucks. But his intensity said otherwise.

Frank counted one, two, three.

We delved into that moment and ran like hell. We broke from the ground, legs pumping, lungs in angry rebellion. The world ignited. The distance of two hundred yards was a thoroughfare, sparkling in afternoon resonance, hellish leaves like ticker tape, and the faraway fence was jeering at us. For once, the clocks moved neither forward nor backwards, the moment a singular point of light. He immediately jumped out in front of me, boots and all. He took long leaping strides that were impossible to match. Along with his philandering and gambling and whatever else he did, I guess he was at one point also a goddamn alternate sprinter. Frank was way more than a nose ahead, making no contest of it. We beat against the wasted ground, bounding toward the fence, fists and blood impelling us forward, hurtling past sound so that the mad propulsion eradicated all but the resounding thump, thump, thump of heartbeat and stampeding feet, joined by the intense heat and failure of muscles.

I strained every bit of energy and strength, one of my legs was beginning to cramp. I was so completely outmatched that I finished the run with more of a walk.

The fence was my support and comfort. Frank lit a cigarette, apparently unfazed by the match.

"You owe me a hundred bucks," he said.

I laughed. "You must be f-ing kidding. You set me up. That was bullshit."

"And also, you can say 'fuck' with me."

"Ok, then you must be fucking joking."

"I am not joking. You agreed."

"I know that I agreed, but that was a set-up."

"Good. Then you owe me for your second life lesson. You owe me a hundred-dollar fee," he said.

I was confident that this was not the emergency that Will was cautioning me about and that I was going to have some explaining to do. I pulled the bill from my wallet and held it out to Frank. He didn't take the bill. He smoked and stared into the deep shadows that were now encroaching on us. He had gotten nowhere with me, except to swindle me out of a hundred dollars.

"That was a sweet con," I said.

"A hundo," he said, "That was the agreement."

"Here, take the goddamn money," I said. "Take me back. Please. Linda said before dark."

"It's only one? Ain't dark for another three hours."

"I don't see the point in all of this."

"That's the problem."

"The problem is that you tricked me. You are just like they said you would be."

This seemed to hit a nerve with him.

"Apples and foot races," I said. "Take me back please. I need to study."

He stood motionless. "Maybe they conned you. Maybe you conned yourself."

"What is that supposed to mean?"

"You can go home if you want to. I understand. You don't know me, and truthfully, I don't know any of this," he said, waving his hand toward the apple field. "I only know that it seems like this is what people do on Thanksgiving. Is it?"

I shrugged my shoulders.

"Or is it that they make pies. Roast turkeys and shit." He inhaled deeply, staring at the distant hills as if an answer may come from there "Never welch on a bet, Brogan. It's bad business. Trust me. Try to figure the odds first, and then bet decisively. And don't be a sucker. Today, you were a pigeon. I made you a pigeon, and you went along."

"A bird?"

"Easy prey. What are you even doing here in the first place?" he asked.

"You asked me to come here," I said.

"I'll tell you what. You can fork over the hundred bucks and we're square or you can take a ride with me. I have some business to take care of. We can get to know one another."

"Frank, I can't go with you. You heard what Wlll and Linda said."

"That's the point."

"You don't understand. You don't know my parents."

"I know them better than you think I do."

"I'm just starting to think that this is one big mistake."

"Well, that is perfect. That is it precisely. Accidents make people. Maybe you need to stop being perfect and make a few mistakes. They're fun."

"I don't really know what that means. It's been a real hoot. Thank you. I'm glad that we got to take this outing. But really I should be going back."

Don't be such a pussy. I could hear Dan's voice.

"Ok," Frank said. "I'll take you back."

He turned and walked toward the fence line where the Chevy was parked.

I **HADN'T GONE AT** *first. I even skipped a few of our 'weekends'*
that were hers.

The 163 across town was practically empty, and the hiss of air
conditioning drowned out the shifting gears, the bopping of tires,
and the rattle of light conversation. From the muffled cabin of the
bus, the framed town passes by in blurred, silent montage. When
the bus stopped at a light or intersection, the world was suddenly
jarred into stark portraits of constancy. Summer camps were busy
with children in lollipop colors, with the monkey bars strangled with
tanned bodies, and the young aides in white caps and shirtsleeves,
herding and directing the colorful waves across the brightening, clean
summer park. The gas station lines stretched to the street with vans
and convertibles that were jammed with Jersey Shore-destined beach
chairs. The normalcy was sickening. Finally, we drove past the dime
stores, the Italian delis of Anderson Ave, and the bakery that sold
bread from the side door at four in the morning. The White Castle
hamburger joint, with its faux whitewashed turrets, was the final
landmark before ascending the steep hill to the next town, where tall
buildings spiked at the morning sky.

I stood outside the apartment, a nondescript towering brick ten-
ement with windows thrown wide open to the traffic clogged streets.
The garbage near the curb had grown considerably. A mosaic waft

of spaghetti sauce, curry, and fried chicken floated from the open windows.

My Sunday clothes waved any thought of suspicion. I slipped past two black teenagers with a basketball, who gave a quick look, shrugged, and skipped down the stairs. The walkup of three floors was choked with a thick cloud of sweated bodies, and down the narrowed hallway varnished doors lined the paneled walls.

She didn't answer at the first knock. She may have caught the late Sunday Catholic mass. A commotion of chains and locks brought the door open. Linda was mussed in a bathrobe with absent eyes. She stared for a moment, and then left the door open.

"I thought it was next weekend," she said. She smoked a cigarette and fixed a cup of coffee.

"It is," I said.

"It's not like I even expected you to show up."

I wished for the spaghetti sauce smell to have come from her apartment. I wanted that grease drift of frying meatballs in the air, and the lines of sausages, and the escarole soup and the bread with the semolina crust with a soft, brown middle that Will was always crazy about. The kitchen was small with a small electric stove that was cluttered with crusty pots. The metal table was busy with dirty cups. A steeple of butts rose from a full ashtray. A cardboard pizza box was filled with unfinished crusts. It was late August, and the heat was growing into the kitchen.

"It's not that I'm not happy to see you. I'm glad you're here."

"When did you start smoking again?"

"This is nothing. Passing the time, and don't be so judging. I just wish," She released the smoke out the window onto the fire escape, "I just wish that you would call sometimes before you came. Your father will be looking for you."

"And eat pizza now?"

One of her bras was looped over the kitchen chair. She had become all too human to me. The kitchen led to a small living room with an unused television set and a coffee table tangled with summer seminar essays. The place was a disaster.

My mother was demanding when she was at home, marshalling me with detailed lists in her looped handwriting, and securing notes with orders beneath a magnet on the fridge: "1. Dust the frames. 2. Vacuum the liv room/ din room 3. (For the love of Christ) General Tidying!" She moved through the rooms of our home with monologues on the state of dirt and filth, a washcloth fixed to her hand and broom in the other as if they were part of her anatomy, pausing regularly to complain to a portrait of Jesus that hung in her bedroom. "Give me strength, Lord. I don't want to murder all of them."

"Take your blessed shoes off," she would say to Dan all the time. She was never a big fan of Dan. She said that he reminded her of someone she would like to forget. "This place looks like Hester Street," she would conclude to us, her two-person, thoroughly entertained audience.

"Where's Hester Street?" I would ask, generating a rise out of her that was short of a broomstick up the ass.

"Damn, if my house was this clean, my mother would take pictures!" Dan would say, which would throw her into a full-blown maniacal rage, wielding her broomstick, and threatening to brain me and Dan, and of course, thanks to Dan's genius, extricating me from any further chores.

That embedded desire for exactness was lacking greatly in her own space. Coffee stains were ringed on the end table. Unlaundered sheets lay in a heap near the bedroom door, and the sunlight revealed a fine layer of dust on the lampshade.

"Let's have lunch then," she said.

She disappeared into the single bedroom, leaving me to the mess. I took the time to look around the rest of the apartment. A healthy stack of books sat on her desk. She always took great care in selecting novels for her Women's Studies group.

She returned wearing a light summer dress. Her hair had grown and fell past her shoulders, and she looked much younger and refreshed.

"What?" she said.

"You look pretty amazing," I said.

"You say that in a strange way,"

"I'm not sure how I mean it,"

She called for a cab, and we waited downstairs. My Sunday tie was thrown over my shoulder. We were silent for most of the ride. I snuck looks at her, amazed at just how attractive she was. Despite the crowd, when we arrived at the restaurant we were seated immediately.

"I understand they are going to give you a scholarship."

"You understand? Yes, they are. Don't you both talk anymore?"

"Yes. Of course we talk. You're becoming quite a smartass. Watch yourself."

She ordered a Chianti and sipped from it, leaving stains of lipstick on the glass. The smear of red on the rim was weird to me. She was an English professor who taught in bunned-up hair and unflattering suits. She didn't wear lipstick. She didn't drink. This ersatz professor prettied her hair and lip-sticked her drink. She was new and unshackled and had more light in her eyes.

The old neighborhood trattoria was sectioned with long tables with red and white tablecloths. Clutches of neighborhood men crouched at the corner tables and sipped at cappuccinos. Guests were coupled with other guests to accommodate the swelling of the after-church crowd. We were seated across from one another at the far end of a picnic-styled table. A disinterested waiter hurried a verbal menu, and we settled on a starter of carpaccio and then the veal. I wanted her homemade Sunday dinner, not this impersonal meeting with my mother's wine and her newfound accessories.

Just then two younger well-dressed men entered. They were seated by the host at the opposite end of the restaurant. They unraveled their silverware and took up their napkins. Without an order, the waiter smiled (his first unforced expression) and delivered two grappa.

One of the seated men was dressed in a summer-weight tan and well-fitted suit. He had a too clean face. He looked over, searching for the waiter, raising his hand for attention, and then, recognizing my mother, smiled and nodded with a light of recognition. She looked away.

"Did you go to mass today?" my mother asked.

"I left after communion," I said.

"You're not supposed to leave until the priest gives the final blessing."

"Did you go?" I asked.

"I don't want you taking the bus on your own anymore. Wait until your father can drop you off. I don't want to say it again."

When the waiter appeared, she ordered another Chianti.

"Now, you smoke and drink wine. This is interesting."

A half-smile, somewhat tragic, came over her, and for an instant the sleep-stained blotches of worry that were all too familiar in the days before she left home returned and dragged beneath her eyes. "You know how long it's been since I could have a glass of wine?"

"How long is this going to last?" I asked.

The well-suited man rose and took some effort to angle around the tight quarters of the back-to-back patrons. He stood upright and smiled down on the two of us. His dark curled hair fell out at the end with a single loop that strategically dropped toward his designer glasses. He was fresh-faced and brightened with a clean shave. A single mole was just below his chin line, the only break in a flawless design, and a perfect target for a left hook. He offered his hand to my mother with so much élan that I figure he must have watched a lot of goddamn movies. "Miss Camden."

The murmur of the café was silenced. Miss?

"It's unexpected, but pleasant to see you here today," he said.

She didn't answer directly but nodded in sheepish recognition. She belted a good slug of the Chianti and met my eyes.

"This is my son," Linda said.

"Pleased to meet you," he said. The conversation was halted there. He danced a nervous tap on his mirrored shoes, searching. "Alphonso is in the kitchen today and you would be hard pressed not to have the Ossobuco."

"Thank you, Sergio," she said. "We've ordered."

"Right. All the best then," he said and paused. "Enjoy," he concluded. He left then and sipped at his grappa. I caught my mother sneaking a glance at him using a mirror on the wall.

"So, when do you start at Seton? I can come and get you and we can pick up the uniforms," she said.

"Sounds good," I said.

We ate in silence through the carpaccio, and the veal, and in the end, we shared a coffee, until at last, a slice of tiramisu, which she left untouched.

"So, how is he?" she asked.

"You know," I said, "I think we can skip the trip for the uniforms. We've already got it covered with a tailor. It will save you the ride over."

"And your books and your class schedule? I need to pop over there."

The two men were now paying their bill, and stood at the door talking with the manager of the restaurant

"Is he still at it?" she asked. "I worry."

"Well," I said, forking up the last of the dessert with a mild buzz settling on me from the liquor-soaked cake, "I'm certain he's probably going to shoot our neighbor. Or himself. Or someone for that matter."

"I'll take the check," she said, the darkness coming over her again, stealing away her Sunday, lip-sticked costume.

"You don't have a check," the waiter said, half smiling, half annoyed at the threat of his missed tip.

"*Who the hell was that guy?*" *I asked. He was still looking over at us.*

"*He's a friend of the family,*" *she said exasperated, and she seemed somewhat frightened.*

"*What side of the family?*"

"*Your father's.*"

"*How is he related?*"

"*He's an,*" *She searched for the right word.* "*Acquaintance? Of your Uncle Frank.*"

"*No shit,*" *I said.*

"*Don't swear,*" *Linda said.*

IT WAS AFTER five P.M. when Frank and I stopped at a highway rest station just off the New Jersey Turnpike. Frank refilled the Chevy with gas, and we ate cheeseburgers with fries near the picnic table. The lot was filled with holiday travelers. Frank chewed on his burger and sneered. He fixed an uncomfortably prolonged stare at the female bottoms, shook his head, and then laughed.

"I think sometimes these birds flock together to avoid predators," he said. "Like me."

The rest stop was unusually busy for this time of night. I had to use the bathroom, and Frank told me to be wary of "the fruits that hang around the bathroom trying to take a flick of your noodle." It took me a minute to decipher his language.

Frank was right. It was a strange place, almost like a waiting spot between worlds. The cars circled in from the highway, and the bodies emerged from the shadows and into the light. Maps of New Jersey were posted next to a welcome station that was closed for the upcoming holiday. I stopped at the bathroom but didn't go in. I went to the burger shop and ordered us two burgers and two coffees, and asked the cashier (as per Frank's instruction) to give me ten dollars' worth of quarters.

When I returned, Frank was seated on the hood of the Chevy. I handed him the coffee and the change.

"I want you to take a good, long look at these people," Frank said. "The modern rest stop is a vaudeville theater. A carnival of pain. There are no fixed bridges, Brogan. Remember that. There are no dams."

The cars were heavy with luggage. Mothers barked at their children.

"I hate kids," Frank said. "Always screaming and yelling and leaking shit out of their faces. Nothing that a good tire iron couldn't handle," he added.

"You were a kid once. Yes?" I asked.

"Never."

The burgers were gone, and just as fast, Frank was smoking. He pulled a notebook from his back pocket and made a few calculations.

"What's that?"

"It's a notebook," he said.

"I understand that, but what do you use it for?"

"I write things in it."

"What things do you write?"

His eyes stared upward, as if pondering the question. "Well, the Brits would say that I'm a punter."

"Like football?"

"Yeah. I would say that football is sometimes a part of it."

"Ok," I said. "So – how is punting a part of it?"

"You ask a lot of questions."

"You talk in riddles."

"I examine the possibilities of situations. I use evidence to realize potential eventualities. Then I decide."

"What situations?"

"Competitive ones."

"You gamble."

"That's one way of putting it. Housewives and degenerate bankers gamble. Nutritionally starved rubes that know about as much as distinguishing an ass from an elbow. I'm not a tourist, Sport," he said. He licked his finger and paged through the notebook. "I'm a local."

"So, what exactly do you do then?"

"What do I do?" he asked, removing the brown paper bag from his inner pocket, and polishing off the last of the bourbon that he had brought from the apple field.

Frank separated the quarters into one-dollar denominations on top of the ledge of a pay phone. He began to deposit the coins and to dial numbers. He leaned on the pay phone waiting for an answer and looking at me. He put one hand over the receiver.

"Find something to do, and be back here in exactly fifteen minutes," he said.

He began to deposit more coins and dial other numbers. He turned once more to me. "Are you still here?"

I BROKE THE TESTING *curve for the second time in Astronomy and the class was pissed. Professor Wittier wrote the breakdown on the blackboard. I scored a 147 on the test. The nearest grade was 84. The curve had been busted, and the idiots surrounding me were looking over one another's shoulders trying to find the culprit. It wasn't my fault.*

The chess club kids were beside themselves. They were in cahoots, I imagined. The smart kids traveled in herds. They positioned their seats to sit next to one another in all of their high-level classes.

Professor Wittier offered extra credit. I took it. All of it. I wanted all of it.

The football players, who thought studying planets was an easy A, wanted to body-slam someone. If I were visible, they would have known it was me. But I wasn't.

I was wallpaper. Professor Wittier was not stupid. He waited to give me the test paper after the class was dismissed.

"You have a very interesting mind," he said.

Truth be told, Prof, my dad is in an upstate facility drying out, and that gives me about four hours of study time on the way up and back. But thanks!

"Thank you," I said.

I ate lunch by myself on the quad at the Prep on the days when it was sunny. I often found Brother Big eying me suspiciously, and then moving on to pulverize an obnoxious student in the cafeteria.

I didn't have to study anymore to remember what they were saying in class.

People were suspicious of me. I got it. I liked it in a way. One day in history class, Professor Bartelow said that he would excuse the class of weekend homework if anyone could properly spell "bourgeoisie." No one bit. I raised my hand. "B-o-u-r-g-e-o-i-s-i-e." The class was silent. "Very good, Mr. Camden. You can all thank Mr. Camden for the weekend stay of Western Civilization. Enjoy." No one knew who to thank. The suspicion grew. Surely, I was the cocky bastard who kept screwing the curve. Fuck 'em.

On Wednesdays I didn't take the bus. I waited for Linda in the front of the building. She pulled up in an old maroon Plymouth Horizon. In minutes, we were on the highway, past the New York City-bound traffic, and heading toward the country fields of western New Jersey. She sang softly along with the radio. She always waited for me to want to talk first.

"I broke the curve again," I said.

"Good," Linda said.

The car overheated twice on the way to the facility. We followed a winding country road to the Sunrise House, an inpatient facility on top of the hill that looked like an old estate home. Skeletal trees lined the pathway toward the top. A statue of Mary was outside the front door. It should have been comforting, but it was more ominous. She had blanked out eyes, and her hands were thrown in the air as if she were blind and trying to find her way. We checked in, and the staff person removed the mouth wash and the hair spray from Linda's purse. We weren't allowed to bring anything inside that included any kind of alcohol. Still, I couldn't imagine someone downing a shot of hairspray.

After we checked in the staff called upstairs to let Will know that we had arrived. Linda dressed her best, and she caught more than a few looks while we waited.

Will came down from a long hallway, dressed neatly in slacks and a button-down shirt. He was in a crowd of gaunt heroin addicts, cocaine addicts, methamphetamine users, and other alcoholics

Will looked good. Strong. The man I had known my entire life. He sat down and took charge. He discussed the household with Linda. They held hands. I had never seen that before. When they were finished, he turned to me.

"How's school going, kid?" Will asked.

I didn't answer.

"I asked you a question, boy."

"It goes."

"Are you being a smartass with me?"

"There isn't much to say, Will."

"Well being a mute isn't going to get us anywhere."

The last time that I had seen Will he was emptying the liquor cabinet at George McConnell's annual nutcase Labor Day party. Our neighbor's dog had shit on our lawn again, and Will had decided that was enough pay him a visit with a loaded nine-millimeter. Every police car in three towns arrived on the scene. Will didn't fight them when they tried to take the gun, but six police officers could not wrestle him into the back seat.

The sky was late summer orange, and the lights of the siren barked a carnival burlesque against its fading backdrop.

Will relented and eventually rode shotgun with the chief. I waited at home until someone had the bright idea to call Linda.

That was it. Either go to rehab or lose his job.

I had only seen him one Wednesday since that whole shit show went down. Linda had returned to the house and was busy getting the place back in order. She surrendered her apartment and decided to come home and stay with me while Will recovered. It was a disaster.

And now he wanted to know how I was doing.

I was as fit as a fucking fiddle.

RETURNED TO THE phone booth just shy of fourteen minutes. Seton Prep was big on the idea of being early for an appointment. Frank was finishing up the call, with the phone in his one ear, and trying to balance the notebook on the shelf.

"You ready for this?"

"We should just go. Why do I have to call?"

"It's the responsible thing to do."

"You must be kidding me," I said.

"I am not kidding with you. Make it quick. We got a boatload of driving to do."

Frank handed me a quarter and waited outside the phone booth while I made the call. So what if they decided to send an army after me. The line picked up on the second ring.

"I give you twenty minutes," Linda said. "And then I'm reporting an abduction."

"It's just for tonight," I said.

"Brogan, don't you feel that you are risking everything? We have worked so hard. We made a deal. Home by sundown. It's now sundown. And you are not here."

"Frank says that we are going to a party."

Silence. I could only imagine the ten thousand scenarios that were going through her head.

"This is insane. You talk to him," Linda said, and I could hear her passing the phone to Will.

Will came onto the phone and was all business. "Put Frank on the phone. Now."

"Will, let me explain," I said.

"Now," he said. "And stop calling me Will."

Frank took the receiver. I could hear Will raise his voice on the other end. Frank nodded his head for a moment and then placed the phone into the cradle while Will was still speaking. He looked at me and smiled.

"Well, I guess this is it. You can ante up or you can pay the vig. It's your decision," he asked.

A **DUSTING OF SNOW** *came that morning. Will left early for an Alcoholics Anonymous meeting at the church and was back before breakfast. Linda drank her coffee. She had called in for the day, and her classes were being covered.*

"I'm just having trouble wrapping my head around the whole thing," I said to Linda. I joined her at the kitchen table. I didn't want the plate of pancakes that she had made me.

"You should eat. It's been days," she said.

Linda was dressed already in a black suit. Her hair was tied conservatively in a bun. Will joined us, also in a black suit.

"I'm not sure that I want to go," I said.

"I understand," Will said. "That is your decision and I support you either way. But we are going to pay our respects."

I got dressed and we made it in time for the first showing. The streets were twisted with cars, and we had to park and walk a good distance to the funeral home. The line was already extending around the block, and I could recognize students from Ridgefield High. I saw an old girlfriend of Dan's, one of many on the line, and she was crying. Laforte was there also dressed in a suit, and Andrea in a black dress.

"Can we just drive around the block," I said. Will pulled out of his hard-earned parking spot and drove around.

Linda stared out the window. She reached a hand behind the seat and held mine. We circled back around. Will was able to park closer. We took our place at the back of the line. Everyone was there: Ridgefield High School, Seton Prep, The Department of Public Works, the Fire Department.

The cool air was gone. The room was milky and hot. The men kept their jackets on. At the front of the room, I could see Dan's head propped above the casket. He had stubble on his chin. It would continue to grow. His face was bloated. He was wearing his Misfits shirt and his denim jacket, and his hands were crossed over his chest. I stared down on his lifeless shell, his closed eyes. The mortician got his smirk right, twisted just a bit up to the right. This couldn't be right. None of this made sense. I looked to Dan's brothers, a line of bearded and older men, broken on the chairs. They faced the casket like Dan's last audience.

Andrea was seated next to me. I smelled her perfume and she put an arm around me.

I let her keep it there.

I sat for a long time. The crowd thinned. The flowers lined both sides of the casket. They were going to put my friend into the frozen ground. I was still waiting for the joke to be over. The idea of Dan dead was foreign and confusing. They would fill the hole and then slap a concrete slab on top of him, and that life, that great force, would be reduced to a name, a birth date, a death date. And the grass would grow back. He would putrefy and his organs would liquefy, and he would turn to dust. I knew, looking around at the blank faces, that in a day or two, in a week, in a year, no one will give a good goddamn about any of it. We had never seen L.A... We had never gone to Paris and dug up Jim Morrison's grave

Outside, the town went back to a November day. Laforte went back to being an asshole. Andrea went back to ignoring me. All had been reset and all was the same.

Linda and Will waited by the car.

"Where were you?" I said to Will.

"I've been here the whole time," Will said.

I left them and walked the rest of the way home.

15

November 26, 1987

Happy 16th Birthday, Brogan.

I hope this letter finds you not a virgin anymore. If that is the case, and you need training or you are frightened, then begin your education with pornography. Don't be ashamed, that is how we all learned. A license means that the road is yours now, and that is the greatest freedom you will ever know. The machines are a part of us inexplicably.

Love, Frank

FRANK DROVE SOUTH as just a shadow in the darkness. The oncoming cars from the northbound lanes illuminated his face, and then it was dark again. The Chevy feasted on the roads, gobbling asphalt highways, red shifting, expanding the universe. Frank appeared and disappeared back into the night. My eyes adjusted to the darkness until the intermittent light redefined him.

It was now ten O'clock somewhere near Atlantic City. At home, tomorrow, the family would arrive for Thanksgiving dinner, suited up and strangled with ties, bulbous dresses and blue hair, with their screaming babies and barking dogs. They would eventually wonder aloud, "Where is Brogan?"

"With Frank!" Aunt Margaret would scream, and Linda would silence her with a stare. But she wouldn't dare bring the avalanche of her anger down on her eighty-year-old Aunt Margaret. Linda would probably be shell-shocked. She never would have imagined it would go this far, just as I never imagined that she could leave Will and me on that day. In the same way that I couldn't imagine her prettied up and drinking her wine and lip-sticking her face, and whatever else she was doing during that time. It wasn't revenge. It was nothing like that. She didn't deserve revenge.

Then the stories of Frank would erupt. The children would be dismissed. With the laughter resounding and the cursing even more abundant, the exaggerated tales would begin with, "Do you remember the time that Frank…" Then the situation wouldn't be as funny. The laughter would turn to concern. Uncle George would hit the Jack Daniels and offer advice.

The car came to a sudden halt, and we were bathed in neon outside of an all-night club gentlemen's club called Scarlett's. Frank flipped on the interior light. He had the notebook out and was blazing through mathematical equations, writing and rewriting numbers.

"What are you doing now?" I looked out the window. Men lined up at the front door and waited to be let inside by two enormous bouncers.

"It's all unscripted theater. Sports. The American addiction."

"What is?"

"I arm wrestle with Fortuna."

He put the notebook down and turned off the car. Outside the muffled music from the club was pulsating the air.

"It may be that predestination denotes that the course of our life is immutable. Salvation is given for some and not others. That doesn't seem too fair. Or even logical for that matter. In other words, you are fucked either way. Born to an endless night. So then, really what is the point in trying? As for the rest of life, I take a dogmatic approach to determine whether all of it is certainty or all probability."

"All of what?"

"Either that massive bitch of a hurricane barreling out of the Gulf is an act of God, (in that case, nothing you can really do about it), or it's a chaotic and somewhat unexplainable event. Or maybe if you dig deep enough, if you got the stones to look further, you can trace it all the way back to the root of the event, to that goddamn butterfly flapping away its goddamn wings in Central Park. The tiniest most seemingly random, seemingly insignificant change that leads to a significantly different outcome. It is then that you have the answers. Do you get it?"

"No."

"What? did you cheat on the S.A.T's?"

He reached over me, opened the glove compartment, and removed only some of a large stack of twenty-dollar bills.

"Either a dog pisses on just any old tree, or some event, some ostensibly prior incident led him to that particular tree. In other words, he pissed on that precise tree for a specific reason: another dog had marked it first, and now he wants to show him who's king shit. Maybe, he smelled some canine pussy? Or it could be as simple as he needed the nearest place to piss. That is the point of all of this," he said holding up the notebook. "It's just that I choose a different avenue to explore those possibilities. And, at the very least, have a sporting chance."

A line of cars had pulled into the lot, unloading a group of younger men, obviously drunk, who were turned away at the door.

"C'mon. Let's get inside. We have a lot to do in a short period of time."

"What is this place?"

"College," he said, slamming the door, and walking at such a fast pace, that I nearly had to run to catch up with him.

The queue to get inside the club was long. With Frank's influence, we bypassed the wait, and the security man lifted a velvet rope for us. Frank passed him a twenty-dollar bill.

"A good tip," Franks says. "They always remember who gives a good tip. Remember that."

I stood at the portal of a bright, flashing merry-go-round called Scarlett's. They knew that I was underage, but Frank was royalty here.

Inside the club, it was paradise. The lithe bodies of the women were smooth, and there was an aroma of baby powder and perfume. Bubbles of light passed along the wall from a disco ball and danced rhythmically in circles to the music. The air was electric, and the music was loud. The females paraded by us, their breasts and thighs eloquent in their language of milky decadence. For a hormonal, starved adolescent, the club was overwhelming. The whole scene was terror and ecstasy all at once for me and everything swelled, and I was dizzy with the fanfare of lights and music and female nakedness.

A cocktail waitress in dripping straps and silk guided us into the depths, and we descended.

Frank stopped first at the bar and was up on his barstool soapbox citing National Football League statistics like a mathematical professor. Immediately, he met opposition and opposing views. They argued quarterbacks, coaches, defensive strategies. Frank was an encyclopedia.

"He couldn't find a piece a pussy with a roadmap! How do you expect him to make his way of out of the pocket?" Frank asked.

"You know about as much about football as I know about a Chinaman jerking off."

"Well, he does it with both hands and doesn't miss a stroke," Frank replied, "I'll cover action right now on Thursday's contest. Anyone?"

Everyone declined. We moved on.

The lights and the bodies swam and swarmed in on potential monetary targets. How the beautiful bodies contorted and bathed in seesaw light!

I intended to keep busy at that.

"Brogan, for Christ's sake!" Frank yelled, and it seemed like he was a million miles away.

"Frank…," I said, lost and bewildered.

"I know," he said laughing while handing me a twenty-dollar bill. "Give her this, Killer, and then keep walking. We got things to do."

The goddess bent down to me. She smelled like that same perfume and baby powder. She smiled at me and mouthed the words "Thank you." I handed her the twenty.

Well-dressed men sat at the small tables with full bottles of liquor. In the corners of the room, I caught the radiant glow of slithering white flesh easing up and down in perfect liquid motion. Frank slid through the crowd, shook hands, pressed the flesh, and made his rounds. If there were babies in the club, he would have kissed them. When we were seated at our own table, Frank ordered us drinks.

"He's a beer guy," he yelled to the server. "Give him a Budweiser."

She looked at me, then looked at Frank disapprovingly.

"You 21?"

"Yes."

"Of course, he is!"

The server huffed and left to fill the order. Frank handed me yet another twenty.

"Give her that when she comes back," he said and winked.

A procession of managers and dancers and cocktail waitresses passed by our table, wanting to chat and pay homage to Frank.

When we were finally left alone for a moment, Frank snapped his head from one television to the next. His eyes widened with giant pupils, possessed ovals of black that invaded the blue as if he had left and now some demonic entity had taken over. "It's not that I don't do anything, but what I do is hard to put into words. But you'll see it. And when I'm doing it, you'll know."

The stairs led to a central stage which was the main attraction. New dancers arrived on stage after three songs, while the others disappeared into the crowd and into private rooms with pulled shades. On the stage, a woman danced behind a screen so that I could only see her silhouette, and the perfect orbs of her shape.

I couldn't listen to him fully. It was enough for me just to sit still for a moment. Not for a minute would I have departed from that pageant. I was drunk on women. I was drunk on that sweet elixir that dripped from their naked bodies. I was drunk on beer and shamelessly studying the bodies that floated past me.

Frank studied the television with equal intensity. Somewhere in a Connecticut college gym, students were racing up and down a basketball court. His eyes followed the action, and the final seconds of the last quarter were dropping away. From his look, it didn't seem as though Frank was pleased with the result. He had his notebook, that cryptic diary, and he referenced some notes that he had taken earlier.

A man in sharkskin jacket and aqua trousers glided by the table. He walked back and forth several times until he decided to stop. He eyed Frank and pulled up a chair. His face was overly Florida-tan for November, and his hair was perfectly combed back in black and gray streaks. He had a strong chin and nose, and his eyes were sharpshooters. He was a foreigner as much as I could tell by his brilliant white shoes. I'm guessing somewhere in Latin America. He was overwhelmingly happy to see Frank. Frank slouched in his chair and stared up at him.

"Why is there a kid here?"

"Don't worry about that." Frank skipped a few beats and then said over his shoulder, "Yup. I'll be over in a minute."

At the bar, three other large men were watching the conversation, one, a man in a black turtleneck with a huge barrel chest and white hair, and two other giants dressed in serious faces and black blazers.

"Ok, Frank. We see you in minute."

"My nephew," Frank said. He tipped back the bourbon and ordered another with a wave of a hand. "It's my nephew's birthday, and tomorrow is Thanksgiving," he said in a flat voice.

"Your nephew?"

"That's right."

"When you have time, come over and have a drink. You are royalty" He stood to leave.

"I'm fine right where I am for now," Frank said.

At the bar, the barrel-chested fellow was tipping back his glass. The three large men looked like triplets.

Frank laughed to himself and drank the rest of the entire, substantial glass of bourbon. I picked up the glass and sniffed it with its machine oil smell.

"Cocksucking prince." The foreigner was eating away at Frank. He waved over another round for us. "We may need Bogota."

"What's Bogota?"

"A plumber," Frank said.

"A person?"

"Yes, but not in the traditional sense of the word."

I wanted to pursue this with Frank, but the club was hopping again, and the music was thumping, and how could I possibly think of plumbers and strange fellows in fancy jackets when I was surrounded by all of this flesh?

Across the room, the basketball game on the television had ended, and Frank shrugged.

"I'll be back," he said and grabbed his pack of cigarettes.

The man in the sharkskin jacket was drinking at the bar with a short, stubby man in a fedora and bow tie and the three natty giants. Frank had a brief but seemingly fierce conversation with them. The manager who had approached us earlier was at the bar immediately and parting them with hands. He flashed a nervous smile. With one look from the three men, he was dismissed easily.

I sidled up to the bar, squeezing next to a topless woman who was sitting on the lap of an obese man with a large cigar and a horrific and inaccurate shave. After several attempts to get his attention, the bartender stopped cleaning a glass and leaned in to hear me.

"Bourbon."

"Oh, yeah?" he said.

"Yes, please."

"Kiss my ass," he said and walked away, laughing.

Back at the table, Frank had a collection of strippers like stuffed animals, white foxes with big button eyes, beautiful and silky to the touch, but empty. They had taken over the chairs. Frank had a dancer on each of his legs and he was smoking a cigar.

He signaled me over. I ducked my ear close to hear him.

"We're going to have a little pit stop," he said around the cigar clenched in his teeth. "No worry. Gonna be quick. Are you in?"

"Yes."

"Good. Still scared shitless about Will?"

"Yes."

"That makes two of us," he said. "We will be reinvigorating the coffers." He shifted one of the strippers off his lap and onto the couch, "Excuse me for a second, ladies. I need to speak with my nephew." The girls fixed a drink from a bottle on the table and moved on.

Once again, he was fixated on the television. "Basketball. I should have my head examined! Too dependent on delicacy, on personality. A game of stars. Divas. You understand?" He sat back and looked toward the other set of television screens. "Football – that's scientific. Math. The individual in service of the team. The collective. Precise algorithms of cuts and patterns, of blocks and tackles. No freelancing."

Frank leaned back and pulled on his smoke. "I do believe that I see a dog track somewhere in our future though. That's your advance education. Your doctorate. In the meantime, I need to work a bit tonight. Have you ever seen Atlantic City?"

"No, never."

"Well, tonight you will. And, in the meantime, I have a present for you. After all, it is your birthday soon."

As if on cue, she floated from across the room and arrived in all her perfection: the slope of her shoulders, her breasts wonderful globes, propped and attentive, and her stomach a smooth, muscular passage down to her scant underwear. On her ankle was a tattoo of a rose with a dragonfly above it that was forever poised to take flight. She chatted with Frank and then sat on my lap. She had the scent of a candy store. She smiled, and that smile made the world cave in.

"Mia, this is my nephew, Brogan," Frank said.

She stood and pulled at my hand and arm.

"Where are we going?"

"A birthday gift," Frank said. "Happy Birthday."

"Come with me, sweetheart," she said.

I was scared, and for the first time, I wished for my home and my bed. "I don't want to go," I said, laughing, trying not to insult her.

"You'll have fun, baby," she said.

"Go," Frank said.

"No, thank you," I said.

"Frank?" she asked.

"Go on, kid—the moon and the stars!"

What the hell did that mean?

"No, thank you."

She conceded. "It's okay, Frank," she said. "Maybe later?"

"Go!" Frank said. "Trust me, Brogan. You want to do this," he said and turned away.

As we left, Frank inclined more toward the television, and he removed his notebook. I looked once more over my shoulder and saw Frank walking toward the three men at the bar. I guess he needed a tree to piss on. Mia and I passed through a dark tunnel and entered the third door on the right, a private room with a loveseat. Mia instructed me to sit down and relax. The secret chamber was calming, but the music was incredibly loud and rattled the furniture

"First time?"

"Does it show?"

"Frank is quite the character."

The next song began, and she began to sway with it and she put both hands on my shoulders, and her beautiful face was only inches from mine.

"You don't have to do this."

"Relax honey."

"I am relaxed."

"No, you're not." She smiled and her one hand slipped down between my legs. I nearly leaped through the roof.

"Ha. Ok. Ok. Just calm down."

"I'm sorry."

"Don't be."

"You don't really have to dance. We could just talk for a while."

"That would be nice," she said. "It's on Frank's dime, and you have as much time as you like to do whatever you like with it." She went over to the table where there were cocktails waiting for both of us.

She brought me one, and one for herself.

She lounged on the couch and curled her legs to her chest. When she relaxed and was away from the stage, she looked more like a teenager than a stripper. She looked like one of the girls who may have passed me along the corridors of a Catholic high school.

"So, how is your little trip going?" she asked.

"A bit strange, I would say. How do you know my uncle?" I asked.

"He's been coming here for years. Everybody knows him. It's like a second home."

She waited for me to continue the conversation. "You don't really know how to talk to girls do you?"

"No. Not really."

"You want to say something complimentary first. But don't be a jerk about it."

"You are very pretty."

"Not bad. A bit general and vanilla. You want to be original, but not a creep."

"You have great ears."

She laughed. "Well, that's a first."

"I mean it," I said. My stomach was doing back flips.

"Ok. Thank you."

"They are small and functional, and they are hidden in your hairline, like someone who is shy but afraid to come out from behind the curtain. But there is a softness to them, and you don't even need those earrings, and even though you are incredibly beautiful, that is the only place to reach you."

"Wow," she said. "A poet."

Now I really felt like an idiot.

"That was wonderful. Usually it's the eyes, or the hair, or the smile, or my tits," she said thrusting her chest toward me. "I like yours the most."

"So now what?"

"Now you want to ask the girl something about herself."

"How old are you?"

"Nope. No way. Never that question. Never ask a woman if she is pregnant, and never ask a woman her age."

"Ok. So how do you know my uncle?" I said again, desperately trying to change the subject.

She stood and went to a side table and pulled a pack of cigarettes from the drawer. "A while back, he got me out of my mother's house and into beauty school. I just trusted him."

She lay back down and put her head into my lap. She took my hand and put it on her soft hair and began to move it back and forth. Sweat was collecting on my back and running in cold streams.

She closed her eyes, and I ran my fingers through her hair.

"Are you guys close?" she asked.

"I suppose. But in a weird way," I said.

The silence was killing me. I didn't know what to say next.

"I wonder what it's like to have family like that." She sighed and shifted her small weight. "A hundred years ago, when my father was still alive, things were different. I was actually part of a family. He worked for an elevator company his whole life. Once, when I was really little, he took me to one of the really tall buildings in the city. It must have been the Empire State Building. I asked him where the elevator was taking us, and he told me 'to the stars.' It really did feel like heaven up there, just me and him above the whole world, and that odd sort of quiet. When he was forty-nine, he dropped dead of a stroke and left us a shitload of money. We never knew he had all that money. In that one year, my mother became a pill head and a gambler. One year. We lost everything. Another small-town heartache. Huh?"

"You did what you had to."

"I am more than this, you know."

"I know you are."

"Yeah, but Frank liked me because I wasn't like the rest of these waifs. Pilled out and pulling an abortion every other week from screwing one buck to the next. He said I was like a blue period Picasso. I never knew what that meant. So, one day I grabbed a bus and went to the city, and I saw those paintings. I had to stare at them for a while to get it. I'm not used to that sort of thing. I'd never even been in a museum before. Frank was right. I could see myself in those sad paintings. I wasn't insulted. I guess I am a little blue. Anyway, he didn't want me here in this place. He wouldn't let me dance for him. In fact, I don't think that I've ever seen Frank take a dance." She shot up quickly. "Do you want to hear something crazy?"

"Yes, I do."

"I found out years later that he wasn't even my real father. But he was. As for my mother, she become one of those Jehovah's witnesses. And, you know how that goes. So, I guess I hung on to Frank here and there."

She picked her head up from my lap again and became very serious. "Do you know how to kiss a girl? That's usually the next step. The one that comes after the compliment, and the small talk. And, probably the most important step of all."

"I suppose." I had fumbled though many kisses with Andrea. She knew that I had no experience, and she was real pain in the ass about it.

"Stand up." I stood up. "Now say the thing about my ears again." I did. "Now move close and put your palm on the side of my face." I was terrified but did what she said. "Now look into my eyes." That was the hardest part. "Don't look away." I brought my gaze back to her eyes. "Now, relax. It's the hardest thing in the world to stare into someone's eyes for more than a minute." She looked down at a clock. "Ok. Starting now." She stared into my eyes." It was the longest most enjoyable minute. "Ready," She whispered. "Relax." She brought her mouth to mine and for that brief moment the world disappeared beneath me. She pushed me down into the chair.

"That wasn't so bad," she said.

She got into character in front of the mirror. The dance began with the start of the next song. The world was only Mia, silky and dreamlike. Her top was gone. Her panties were removed in a gliding, effortless ballet. She writhed and twisted. Her arms and legs met mine, and her smooth face met mine, resting for a moment, and then her downy skin met mine, and then the divine scent of her hair. I was crossing over, and there were no longer any definitive boundaries between us.

Happy Birthday Brogan!!!

All that you know and all that you will ever be. One day you when you read this, and when you can, know this, if only this: the countdown begins on this day. The moon and the stars! They are yours now. Someday, someone, somewhere, will ask you to give them away. Hold fast. Make your decision as to whether it is yours to part with, and if so, whether you are willing.

Love, Frank.

*O*N THOSE NIGHTS *years ago in New Jersey when Linda was away, Will would drink at the kitchen table and always with the lights off. In that darkened cave, the past drifted by Will in shadows of delusion, of what was real and what was not, or what appeared to be real, that continuous parade of images that marched across his swelled mind and flowed from his conscious, onto his tongue, and into my space, leaving me with questions of whether these thoughts and these people were tangible or imaginary.*

And, then one night the rain came, a summer storm inhaling the sodden drapes and tapping an increasing drip onto the wooden floor of the bedroom. Across the rooftops of New Jersey, the trees bowed and swung in applause and were ignited in streaks of lightening. I searched the rooms, securing windows against the storm. I found the kitchen was still dark and I could smell the cigarette smoke. The orange glow pulsed, and Will sat at the table, watching the rain fill the room and listening to the wind. The room was empty without Linda here. But her ghost was still there, in the piney, scant fragrance of her perfume, in the evidence of the soapy circles in the bathroom where her shampoo once was.

A Western Union letter sat partially open on the table.

"You been out to see your mother," Will said. I could smell that he had been drinking.

A bottle of whiskey was down a third by now. Whiskey was a dangerous situation with Will.

"We talk," I said, pulling up a chair. "Did she write you a letter, Pop?" I asked.

The cigarette brightened his hardened face. His uniform shirt was open at the collar, and the silvery badge was on the table next to his service revolver.

"I haven't heard from her," he said.

"You should get some rest, Pop," I said.

Will tossed the letter aside and poured another glass of whiskey.

"I worry about him," he said.

"Who's that?" I asked.

"We got tickets for the Mets one time. It was '69. The year they won the series. Tom Seaver was pitching that day. He brought a bottle of Bacardi Rum and when no one was looking he would slip shots into our cokes. Somewhere around the seventh, I fell asleep. Missed almost the whole goddamn game. And, wouldn't you know it? Seaver had a perfect game going. That's like winning the lottery. And then there he was, balls naked, running across the third base line. Security was chasing him around like a circus show. The Cubs were playing that day. I'll be damned if he didn't screw up the whole thing. Jinxed the game. You know what I mean. A goddamn rookie got a hit and blew the game."

"There who was?"

"Frank," he said. "Your Uncle. But that is just the least of it." He got up. "I worry about him."

He left the room and went to the couch. He couldn't bring himself to sleep in the bedroom without Linda.

The Western Union telegram was from Puerto Rico.

We were one in the same on those nights, Will and I, deep in the trenches in a bond of battle. I felt close to him in those moments. Until now, those faces, especially Frank's, were only dreams, masquerade parties of fictionalized people as real or as true as movie actors.

WHEN MIA'S DANCE had ended, I was delirious. I felt the alcohol in its full throttle.

"Come with me," Mia said. She was now dressed. She had left and returned with a winter jacket. She poked her head out of the room and looked both ways, and then she grabbed my hand and led me toward the back emergency exit. We stepped outside into the cold night.

"This is my phone number," she said handing me a small scrap of paper. "This is totally against the rules. Don't be a creep with it," she said. "It's, just that. I don't know. I worry about him."

"Don't," I said. "He would hate that."

"I want you to call this number if you need to."

I caught sight of Frank. He was with the three huge knuckleheads from the club, the skinny foreign guy, and the little imp with the fedora. The trunk of the Chevy was open. They seemed to be still arguing. One of the huge men stepped forward as if he was going to hit Frank, but the foreign guy held him back with one hand. He stepped up to Frank and was counting off one, two, and three, with his fingers. He made sure Frank understood then he turned to leave. He had to practically drag the three goons with him, but they listened and turned and left. Frank closed the door and breathed a heavy sigh.

"What's going on Frank?" I asked.

When he saw me, he was surprised that I was outside already. "Sometimes Brogan, we all have to take our turn on the ass kicking wheel."

"Who are those people?"

"Fortunately, this wasn't my time."

As we drove, the bright headlights of oncoming traffic appeared and disappeared into the night. Frank was translucent. The lines of his face, the deep, wounded wash of his skin was dissolving into nothingness. When the lights captured him in their sights, they made him disappear into a world of gray discontinuity.

We were clear of the strip club and on that lonely stretch of road that led to the interstate.

"Did you bang Mia?"

"Are you serious?"

"That was the test."

"I kissed her."

"Ok. But never bang a stripper, Brogan. I didn't figure you for one who would, but I'm giving you some invaluable counsel here. She will make you feel like Mr. How-Do-You-Do, like you have the one and only golden pecker. The problem is that once you get that on your hands it's almost impossible to wash away. There's much to be learned here though. Christ, she could probably sell the goddamn Empire State Building to a bunch of IRS agents."

We got back onto the highway and headed south. Soon the signs for the Atlantic City exit began to appear.

"That's a pretty broad generalization," I said.

"It's not such a generalization as it is an axiom. You see the thing is they do tell the truth. However, it is only precisely one third of the time."

"That sounds normal for anyone."

"Perhaps. But this is a sure bet. The devil himself is a cute and fluffy doll with big tits, doing the cowgirl. That is until he kicks you in the balls with his spurs."

I rolled down the window, and held my hand outside until it was numb, and let the paper with Mia's number fly into the wind.

WAS DEFINITELY NOT accustomed to drinking as much as we did, or at all for that matter. When we left the club, I already had quite a buzz on. I wasn't sure if Frank knew that human beings actually needed to eat food on a regular basis. We pulled over at an all-night convenience store, and Frank bought a carton of cigarettes, every newspaper that the store had to offer, a case of beer, and some aspirin. He went back for some lip balm, claiming that his lips get dry when he worked. He threw in some pretzels this time. Dinner. Frank had no plans for sleep.

We sat on the curb by the pay phones and ate the pretzels, and Frank smoked his cigarettes. I had the mystic memory of Mia to keep me company. She was too beautiful, almost tragic. No one should have the burden of being that attractive. I believed everything that she said, not just one third of it, and began to regret tossing her number. But, then again, I had the naiveté of a five-year-old.

"Watch out for him," was the last thing that she had said.

"I'll do my best."

"Some of us need him."

I was lost in thoughts of Mia when a Mustang pulled into the lot. The car was crammed with high school kids that were about my age. It was the night before Thanksgiving. Always a big night when students would return home, and everyone would get together again, renew old acquaintances, get piss drunk. I know it was always a big night in Ridgefield, and I always had the pleasure of running into Laforte and Andrea. It was the same here as it was in Ridgefield. Their music in the car was that same droning, synthesized sound and automated beats that Chaz and his friends listened to: The Cars, Frankie Goes to Hollywood, The Fixx. Though the entire lot was empty, they decided to park directly next to the Chevy. This concerned Frank.

Two meatheads with huge shoulders barreled out of the car, their door coming dangerously close to the Chevy. In my head, I had given them both names. Johnny and Bobby. They weren't much different than Chaz, muscled up and stupid and unconscious. Frank was jumpy, having to balance whatever it was *he did*, while entertaining a nephew, and at the same time trying to stave off that ever present monkey. He was in no mood for nonsense.

"Watch the paint, assholes," Frank said, but they were already in the store. Even if they weren't, I'm sure they wouldn't have heard him.

Inside the store, the two meatheads were drifting from aisle to aisle, tossing cans of soda and bags of potato chips back and forth. In the car, the high school girls waited. They had bleached hair, their eyes were snowstorms, their skin a mess of greasy makeup. They giggled and lit cigarettes and pretended to inhale the smoke.

Frank and I watched them from the curb. "This is one thing that I really want you to understand, Brogan," Frank said. "There is a beauty to every woman. I tell you, there is something to love in every one of them. Sometimes it's hard to get past the beauty though. That's why it pains me to see these girls like this. They could be so goddamn precious and beautiful, but instead, they are tracing paper. They will pretend to know what they are doing, and they will spread their legs because they think it is the right and decent and expected thing to do."

"I feel like I'm trying to do the same thing as them, Frank," I said. "Pretty much most of my waking moments."

"I can picture them now. Before going out, they probably bragged to one another while applying lipstick next to a music box that their father had bought for them while he was trying like hell to keep his young girl a baby. They will brag to one another about how they had shaved tonight, and how this is going to be the night, and how these two idiots will be their first and how they are in love, and all that happy horseshit."

"Maybe they are in love," I said.

"I doubt that." he said.

"Why not?"

"Most people don't understand that concept. I'm quite positive they don't. It's beyond their range. It's like trying to define gravity."

"The attraction between two masses."

"Correct Einstein. But what is it exactly?"

"Then why do you tell me to 'use that thing between your legs as much as you can?'" I asked.

"That's for you, not them," he said.

"Well, it seems that it's going to be someone's daughter, some-how, somewhere."

He stopped what he was doing and just looked at me. He seemed frustrated. "I need you to go wait in the car. I have to make a few calls, and then we are back in the soup."

"Do you think that I should call home? Let them know that I'm alright?"

The question was a wound, and he refused to answer. A false smile turned from the corner of his mouth.

"Okay, Frank," I said.

He looked away and slotted the coins into a payphone. I went back to the car, retracing the night and Scarlett's and this crazy road trip. I thought a little about some of the assignments that I had due on Monday. I thought of Andrea with that dickhead Laforte. I sat in the front seat staring off into space, leaning my head against the seat and turning to watch the kids in the car next to me. I didn't realize that I had been staring.

"Hey, Smiley. What you looking at?" the first moron asked me. He was the one that I named Johnny.

"I was looking at your girlfriend," I said.

The beer was talking. The beer had a hell of a lot more to say than I did, and I thought right then, that our short exchange had most decidedly taken a turn for the worse.

You're a scrapper. You just don't know it. And what were they! Look at them, Frank had said.

"What did you say?"

"I was thinking that she looks like a painted ape," I said.

"Oh my God!" the girl screamed as if I had just slapped her.

"I'm gonna tear him a new ass," Bobby said. He was about the size of a Volkswagen.

Painted Ape Number One was howling like I had just run over her dog and Painted Ape Number Two was cheerleading Bobby and Johnny into sending me to the afterlife.

"Are you aware that accidents make—" I began to say.

I tried to get out of the car to further explain the theory when the door was slammed back at me, hurtling me across the front seat. I was then suddenly dragged by my hair out of the driver's side window. I learned that asphalt had a distinct smell when your face is smashed against the gravel surface. Then next came the blunt, blackening blows of two mallets landing on top of my head.

"Elephants and peanuts," I said, and Jesus H., he could hit hard.

And then, the beating had suddenly stopped. Bobby had made a near fatal mistake. He had touched me and more tragically, he had touched Frank's car. Through the black lights that were blotting my vision, I could see that Frank had Johnny by the throat against the Mustang. He was wielding a knife and the shining blade contrasted with the pale neck.

The girls were screaming bloody murder.

"Tell that pain-in-the-ass-bitching-fuck to be quiet," Frank said, pointing one of his pinkies at the screaming Painted Ape number two.

The girls were silenced by Johnny's terrified, pleading eyes. The store clerk came out to inquire about the mayhem.

"Go back inside, lamb chop," Frank said.

The clerk quickly retreated inside, and it looked as though he was making a call. Probably 911. Pulling Johnny close enough to kiss him, Frank said, "Don't make a peep, short stack." It was not often in youth that we see our end. "We understand each other?" Johnny nodded his head. Frank put the knife away. "I hate kids. I hate teenagers even more. The one you're punching over there is the only one I happen to like."

Frank let him go and before Johnny could go, Frank gave him a kick in the ass. "Potato chips and a kick in the ass. Sounds like a better name than Quick Stop. Now, get the hell out of here."

They piled into the Mustang and backed up with screeching tires. Johnny gave Frank the middle finger and they peeled out of the lot.

"Cops will be here in exactly five minutes," the clerk said, then quickly closed the door and locked it.

"We better scoot," Frank said.

There was a bit of blood leaking from my nose, and my head was fuzzy. We got into the car and kept the lights off as we exited the parking lot. Frank looked at me and laughed.

"You have much to learn, young Jedi."

"That was only my second fight," I said.

"Well, I give you a one on a scale of one to ten."

"Room for improvement then?"

"Goddamn right! Fights are not about power or skill; they are about will."

"Oh, Christ, Frank. I don't need any advice right now. Have a cigarette," and we both laughed, and the laughter was free in the blowing breeze of an open car window.

We were covered with sparkles from the strippers and cloaked in their perfume. We shared the same skin now and carved through the night, and the rock music played and screamed. The Chevy rolled on, and it was the early morning of Thanksgiving, and I was certain there would be no turkey. I was definitely still drunk. Frank was conducting songs, moving his arms and head to the rhythm, finding patterns in the rise and fall.

"You should have given me a minute, Frank. I had them right where I wanted 'em."

"Sure did! His fists were getting sore as hell," he said, and the laughter hurt my head and shiny welts were blooming beneath my eye.

"Strange. It doesn't really hurt," I said.

"Sure it does," Frank said. "It's a just a pain that you learn to live with."

BROGAN, WHAT DO you think that they do all day?" Frank asked, once again exiting the hinged door of a phone booth that ended with a loud pop.

"With what?"

"They get up at the ass crack of dawn. Stuff the turkey. Put it in the oven. Baste the damn thing. Break their necks on yams, cream corn, pasta fagioli."

"They don't make that on Thanksgiving."

He paused for a second. "Oh. Well then kielbasa!"

"Mashed potatoes."

"Yes! They spend all goddamn day and all goddamn night overdosing on food. They wake up the next day, and do you know what?"

"What?"

"They shit it all out, a great river of shit, flowing like the Mississippi." He swept his hand across the lot.

"It's more than that, Frank."

"Is it?"

"Maybe they like to see each other," I said.

"Are you kidding? It's only one big morphine shot," Frank said. "I just spoke to your mother and father."

"Holy shit! What did they say?"

"Your father is probably going to put me in the hospital. That's a safe bet. They are calm for the moment." he said, then he cocked an ear toward the sky. "Do you hear that noise?"

"No. I don't hear a thing."

"Listen close," he said, pretending to pay close attention. "That is the sound of your mother cursing me to damnation."

"What did you tell them?"

"I told them that we were on our way back. And then, I heard the distinct sound of Will loading a clip into his nine-millimeter."

"We are going back then?"

He stopped, twisted his mustached and just stared at me. "That's up to you," he said.

"You can't stop a horse halfway through the water."

"Maybe you are smarter than you look."

We sped past the cartooned casino signs of Atlantic City. "Welcome to Atlantic City - America's Playground."

"How come you never came around before this, Frank?" I asked. "You know, for Thanksgiving, or Christmas, or something."

"I was closer than you think," he said.

It was just past 11:00 P.M. when we exited the highway just outside Atlantic City. The pool halls were still open. A pawn shop glowed next to a walk-up liquor store. Drug-addled souls spotted the city streets. Women in stiletto boots and panties leaned in the doorways. A wild, white-heeled pit bull stopped in front of the car and eyed us. The Chevy stopped at a house that mimicked the hundred or so that we had already passed, sullen copies of run-down tenement buildings, low-income cat-walk buildings, broken bicycles crowding the corners, and the vampires hanging from the staircase. The neighborhood was the opposite of my suburban neighborhood, but they may well do the same as any family on Thanksgiving. They will perform the November ritual, get drunk, and shit out Thanksgiving dinner the next day.

While we were waiting outside the house, he wrote in his notebook and rifled through the newspapers from the convenience store by the dome light. He checked the box scores in the sports section and made doodles around the stock prices in the business news.

"What are we waiting for?" I asked.

"Extrication," he said.

It was then that I noticed one of Frank's hands was deformed. His right hand didn't close all the way around the steering wheel. The tips of his ring and middle fingers had been removed.

"Firecrackers?" I said motioning toward his hand.

He gave me an annoyed look and put the hand in his jacket pocket.

"Will always said that could happen. He wouldn't let me have more than a bottle rocket on the 4th of July," I said pointing at his hand.

"Oh yeah," he said. "Firecrackers all right."

A sharp knock rattled the passenger's side window. Frank continued to compute and scribble without looking up. I rolled the window down, not sure what I was seeing.

"Get your skinny ass in the back," the man said.

"Bogota?"

"Sure as shit."

"I'm Brogan," I said, introducing myself and extending my hand.

"No kidding," he said. "But I don't shake hands. Let's go. Move it!" He looked at Frank. "'Misery acquaints a man with strange bedfellows.'"

I recognized the quote from 5th period English. "The Tempest!"

Bogota just shook his head and then motioned me with a thumb into the back seat. He was much taller than Frank and as wide as the Chevy. His shoulders were meaty bulges beneath a T-shirt and a huge leather jacket. His face was strange. It didn't fit the rest of him. He was oddly very pretty and feminine, with almost a woman's fine nose, sculpted in a perfection that nature doesn't offer, a shortened rhinion to a slightly turned up tip. By the bulk of his body, his cheeks should have been fuller, but instead they were high and pronounced, holding high the eyes, with a perfect hollow beneath that caught the night. His lips were full and seemed almost too perfect. They were drawn over crystalline teeth in a snarl that tried to be tough. His jacket sleeves were rolled up, and his arms were hairless. His black hair was long, gathered high in a ponytail like a big pitcher plant. He wore a spicy cologne that smelled like apples. I was positive that he was wearing eyeliner and mascara.

He began by explaining to me the correct pronunciation of his name, which emphasized the O's over the "ta", unlike the phonetic sound of the capital of Colombia. I asked him where he got that name, and he said, "From a cereal box in a train station in Union City."

"That doesn't make any sense," I said.

"Exactly," he said.

"Is that your real name?"

He cast an annoyed glance at me and then at Frank and ignored the question. A duffel bag stretched to the seams was slung over his left shoulder.

"Open the trunk, Frank."

"That's a negative," Frank said.

"Frank! Open the trunk," He held his bag out in front of him and shook it.

"Sorry, Kemosabe. The trunk is off limits."

Bogota tossed the bag in the back seat with a clanking sound, settled into the front seat, and just as fast we were off. Frank squealed the Chevy through the downtown hellish maze of Atlantic City streets.

"Why did they name you that?" I asked, leaning over the front seat.

"Who is *they*?"

"Whoever, your parents."

"I already told you."

"What's your real name?"

"The great inquisitor," he said fixing his hair, and then turning to Frank, "Why does he keeping asking me questions?"

"Stop asking questions," Frank said.

"Pull over here," Bogota said, and Frank steered toward a gas station with a pay phone. The lot was dark and empty. Bogota thumbed a quarter from Frank's ashtray and headed through the knee-high grass to the phone booth.

"Frank?"

"Go ahead."

"Can I ask you a question?"

"You just did."

"About Bogota I mean."

"He's a plumber."

"A plumber? What does that have to do with anything?"

"Let's just leave it at that," Frank said.

Bogota was quick on the phone and brought back with him the night air and that heavy smell of cinnamon apples. He sat for a while, not saying a word.

"Do you want to discuss this here and now?" Bogota asked.

"Are we good?"

"He wants to talk with you."

"About what?"

"It's going to be one hell of a feat to part on 20k," Bogota said.

"I asked for fifty," Frank said.

"Forget it."

Bogota clapped his hands together and laid them onto his lap. He sighed.

"What's the best that we can do?" Frank asked.

"Probably twenty. We are getting two large on five points on the back."

"On a month?"

"On a weekly."

"Well, that certainly is one way to fuck a monkey."

"That's a hell of a mark, Frank. No one wants to do it."

"They owe me," Frank said.

"They do. But that doesn't make much of a difference."

"Christ almighty!"

"Do you want to just forget it, Frank? I make the calls. I don't make the numbers. Oh, and it is due in a month."

"Good Christ, and it's just as sweet as pie from here," Frank said. He lit a cigarette and chewed on his hand.

"Do what you need to do. Just leave me out of this shit this time. Either way," Bogota said. "He's going to want to talk to you."

Bogota indicated lefts and rights through the maze of streets. The light of passing streetlamps were stage lights to Bogota's fine features. The Chevy left the bad neighborhood and moved into a wealthy one, stopping at a big house with tall columns in the front and a long circular driveway. Bogota was out while the car was still moving. He knocked sharply on the front door. A timid and slight man answered the door and was compactly dressed. He admonished Bogota for knocking loudly.

Frank turned to me in the back seat. "Keep this in mind, Brogan. The worst possible thing that you can do is loan money to someone," Frank whispered while watching Bogota. "Sure as shit, it will be the worst thing that ever came to you. And, furthermore, you will be out of friends. Just look at this shmuck!"

Bogota was back in the car. "An even surer road to perdition," Frank said to me, "is to borrow. To borrow is to be indebted, and to be indebted is to be chained to the moon."

"What's a mark?"

"It's a business arrangement. They front me money. I pay it back."

"Isn't that a loan?" I asked.

"Don't get crazy on me, Brogan. This is a business transaction."

"Are you ready?" Bogota asked.

"Yes."

"Leave the knife here."

Frank removed the switchblade from his inner jacket and put it in the glove compartment.

"He's coming," Frank said. He turned off the car and pointed at me.

"No," Bogota said. "He is not."

BOGOTA HAD HIS mouth open in the shape of an "O" while applying a dark pencil onto the outline of his eyes.

"Is that makeup?" I asked.

"It could be," he said, pulling down his eye and coloring the border with a black line. "What did I tell you about the questions?"

"Not to ask them."

"Correct," he said, and went back to darkening his eyelashes.

Frank tapped on the window. "Let's go!"

Bogota's eyes were sharp now and magnetic in the night. The eyeliner was an improvement.

Outside of the car, waves broke against the New Jersey shoreline. The Atlantic City Boardwalk was shadowed near the ocean, and the amusement rides were quiet and dark. But the casinos burned bright. Even at the late hour, crowds of people still moved through the turnstiles and into the fantastical playground of fiery machines and bow-tied, smiling dealers.

"I've never been inside of a casino," I said. I was mesmerized by the bright and blinding lights, the carnival noises, and the sweet scent of flowing champagne.

"Chances are you won't tonight either," Bogota said.

"We are not going in?"

Bogota looked at Frank "Frank is on a time-out."

Frank threw his hands in the air. He was gnawing on the bottom of his mustache. "I got to be lit up better than this."

"That should be the least of your worries," Bogota said.

Frank grabbed me by the jacket and opened the lapels to my Sex Pistols shirt. "Who the hell dresses you?" He looked around the block that was busy with neon storefronts. "We look like a bunch of cafones."

"Speak for yourself there kitten," Bogota said, fixing his long, wavy hair in the reflection of a car window.

Frank scratched his bald head and looked around. "We are not getting anywhere looking like this." He put his hands on his hips and looked up and down the street. "Everything is closed."

"Shocker. It's one o'clock in the morning," Bogota said.

"Fuck me. We need to make an impression," Frank said.

"If you think that is going to help. "

"You still got a bead on Maurice?" Frank asked Bogota.

Bogota shrugged.

"Where the hell was that store?"

"You really want to go that route. No one knows you're in town. Don't you think that we should just keep it that way?"

"I don't see any other choice. Furthermore, l I'm not driving around looking for another goddamn parking space," Frank said and began walking. Bogota followed, and again I found myself almost running to catch up.

"How far to the shop?" he asked Bogota.

"A left at the light, and second on the left."

"Is he still open?" Frank said looking at his wrist that was minus a watch.

"How the hell should I know," Bogota said.

The town was liquor stores and pawn shops. The further that we walked from the casinos, the more dangerous the streets became. Most of the stores had closed already and were guarded by steel gates. Above the stores, apartments were dimly lit, with sheets over the windows. I heard the gruff voice even before I saw the man.

"Get the hell out of here!" he was yelling while shooing away a few prostitutes with a broom. He was a thin man and wearing a Mexican poncho and a rugged cowboy hat.

He looked up once and squinted an eye at us. "Last night, I caught a guy getting a rim job on his ass in the back alley. Every night it's something around here. Who the hell pays for that?" He swept the front of the store. Then, he suddenly looked up again. "Goddamn, Frank. What the hell are you doing here?"

"You still open?" Frank asked.

"You better have money or drugs and by that I mean both."

Once inside, Bogota took a seat in a leopard print chair. He picked an old paperback from a large stack near the window and ignored us for the most part. Maurice locked the door. Frank removed a roll of twenties from his pocket. He took off his jacket.

"No fucking around, Maurice. We have to make this quick."

Maurice had dipped behind a small curtain behind the counter. When Frank said this, he walked back out, holding an espresso pot, and he was now wearing a different hat. It was obvious that he enjoyed reaping the benefits of his store.

"You got some balls on you. I'm not even open. You can take your asses down the road if you ain't got time. This is my show."

"Goddamn it," Frank whispered. "Anything you can do to help this?" He asked Bogota, who just shrugged again and went back to his novel.

Maurice came back out carrying a tray of espresso, and a bottle of Sambuca. He saw the money on the counter. "I see the money," Maurice said.

Without looking up from his novel, Bogota stood, pulled a bag with white powder from his jacket pocket and placed it on the counter.

Maurice disappeared back behind the curtain with the powder. He came back out and was much livelier. He sniffed hard a few times. His eyes were wide. When he took off the hat, he was nearly as bald as Frank. He poured each of us a shot of the Sambuca and an espresso. Bogota drank the espresso, but left the Sambuca, and then sat back down. Frank threw back the shot. I tentatively sipped the expresso. Then the Sambuca. It tasted horrific. Maurice laughed and took my shot.

The overhead track lighting was directed toward a locked case that housed watches and gold and silver necklaces. A camera was pointed at the case with a red blinking light. The room was stacked with every imaginable hocked item. Televisions. Guitars. Saxophones. Piles of silver serving trays. Books. Construction tools. Beyond the merchandise were rows of clothes on hangers. Frank disappeared down the aisles and began to thumb through the clothing on the racks.

"You know that I won't have anything in your size," Maurice said to Bogota.

"Won't need it."

"What about Pip here?" he said.

"Find him something," Bogota said.

"I ain't got new shit back there," he yelled to Frank. "But I do have primo vintage and some swag in the back."

"No time," Frank said.

Frank found a red tuxedo style suit that was in decent condition. "Jumping Jesus, Joseph, and Mary," he said. He looked at the size and checked the length of the slacks against his leg. "This is my size! I've been searching for this my whole life." He disappeared into a back dressing room and pulled the curtain.

Maurice pulled a jacket from the rack and held it up to me.

"I'm not wearing that," I said.

"Used to belong to an Italian barber. Once the monkey got him, he sold me just about everything but his soul. I think Caesar's has rights to that now. See that over there?" he said pointing toward a rack of crammed knickknacks. "That glass right there," he said zeroing in on the glass with a large marble.

"Yes, I see it."

"That's his mother's prosthetic eye. Not worth shit. But I had to have it." He held the jacket close to my chest. "Try this on."

The jacket smelled of aftershave and hair. I removed my jean jacket and slipped my arms into the blazer. The single eye from the glass jar stared back at us. Maurice took a step back and eyed the getup.

"Lift your arms," he said. I lifted them and the jacket flared out. "Plenty of room yes?"

"Yes," I said. "It's huge."

"There has to be plenty of room."

"And it stinks."

"There is always something about formal wear that makes people want to fight," he said. "So, you want to make sure that you have enough room to throw a punch," he stopped speaking and just waited. "Well?"

"What?"

"Can you throw a punch?" Maurice asked.

"You're serious?"

"Yes, I am." He held up his hands like mitts. "Go."

"Go what?"

"Throw a punch."

I threw a punch at his left hand.

"Enough room?"

"I don't know."

"Well, it will have to do. Frank's pants are on fire." He helped me out of the jacket roughly. "You punch like a girl. Now go find a pair of decent shoes that fit you before I decide to sell you a dress instead."

Frank was then emerging from the curtained room. He was dressed in a red tuxedo with a silvery stripe down the side.

"You look like the Jackson Five," Maurice said.

"Never mind him," Frank said. He looked at the jacket. "It will have to do. You got to understand something Brogan. You always want to look the part. It's the first thing they will notice about you."

"Who?"

"Everybody."

Underneath the red jacket was a sharp white shirt. He was looking the part of James Bond, if that was what he meant by that.

"You have to own it," he said to me "You have to live it. Then and only then will they believe it," he stood in front of a full-length mirror and adjusted the pants, "and then they will believe only if you believe it." He bent down and polished a pair of white shoes. "Figure out the play, and what is your part." I looked once more at that maniacal suit. And, yes, it was certainly him. And, yes, Frank owned it.

I went to the back and changed into the suit. It was a size too big. So were the shoes. I looked like Charlie Chaplin. Bogota looked up once from his book. He gave me the once over, shook his head and went back to his book.

Frank held up his roll of twenties.

"It's covered," Maurice said. "I'm guessing you're in on the game at Fin's?"

"That's right. What do I owe you?"

"Frank. I couldn't charge you. You are a prince around here." Maurice held up both his hands to ward off the money. "How's your father?"

Frank stopped what he was doing, placed both hands on the counter and stared directly at Maurice. "Well, I guess he must be the king."

"It's just a question," he said.

Frank peeled off one hundred dollars and laid it on the counter. He gathered up his change of clothes. Bogota folded the novel and left through the door. Frank never broke the blank stare that he gave Maurice as we exited.

We stood outside of Lucky Fin's, a bar and pool hall, a building that stood like a mistake in that neighborhood, flanked by a gun store and an abandoned laundromat. Frank unlocked the back of the trunk and looked inside. He held up a hand for Bogota and I to stay put where we were. He took out a gym bag. He closed the trunk and checked to make sure it was locked.

"Showtime," Frank said.

Inside, the tables were crowded, and clouds of cigarette smoke drifted toward the ceiling. The place reminded me of an old Veteran's of Foreign Wars Hall. A long dusty bar was along the wall. The back of the hall was sectioned off into what I imagined was once a banquet hall. We moved into the darkness. Both the men and the women stole glances at Bogota and then Frank in his nutty suit, and then me, looking like a recently released prisoner. Maurice was also along for the ride. He was now also dressed in a suit. The cowboy hat was replaced with a bowler hat. He smoked a cigarette from a holder. He had a silver flask.

"Some things you just have to see for yourself," Maurice said. "Besides, rumor has it that you're hot right now."

The bartender gave him a familiar salute. Frank's walk was purposeful down the aisle toward the back room. His bald head gleamed ahead of us like a light house. Bogota and I followed through the maze of pool games.

A black man guarded the room at the back. He was tall, with tremendously big arms like sledgehammers hanging off his shoulders. They didn't fit his body. They weren't fit for the body of a mere mortal. He moved slow and languid. He lazily left his stool and approached Frank. Bogota and I wait near the door.

"You got no allowances here," he said to Frank. His eyes were droopy and bored, and he looked everywhere, except at us.

"But I'm already dressed."

"No kidding," he said. "All *Soul Train*. Still don't make a difference."

"Do you even know who this man is?" Maurice asked.

"A word with you," Frank said to Sledgehammers.

"C'mon man, you know the situation."

Frank took a step forward and spoke into the big man's ear, then showed him a wad of money.

"You know it ain't my call, Frank," he said. "I got people to answer to." Sledgehammers' eyebrows raised up, the only expression of emotion that he showed.

He looked to the back of the room, where a man in a green leisure suit waved him on. "I suppose that changes things," Sledgehammers said. "Looks like you got a pass," he said.

Frank took out another five twenty-dollar bills rolled them together and handed them over.

"I miss you," Sledgehammers said and pocketed the money.

Frank entered that sectioned off room near the back of the bar. I stepped forward and got my first look at that back room. It was much larger than I expected, and not much different than the casino that we had just passed earlier. Along both walls, bright and colorful gaming machines were ringing and making festive sounds. A runner boy was hustling around the room delivering sandwiches and cocktails to well-dressed men that were seated at card tables. The only women in the room were gathered around the roulette wheel.

At the table near the back exit, I saw the Latino man from Scarlett's in his blue pants and white shoes. He stood and hugged Frank. Five other card players were seated with them, including the other large fellows from Scarlett's. They smoked foreign cigarettes, and they blurted in their guttural language. A shorter, strange fellow with a bow tie and a fedora hat stared at us like he was picking pastries in a bakery. Bogota sneered at him. The man scoffed, crossed his legs, put his out-of-place umbrella on a folded newspaper, and returned to the business of rearranging his chips.

Sledgehammers sauntered back toward the door. He looked up over our shoulders toward a clock and didn't make eye contact.

"Players only," he said and breathed an annoyed sigh.

"I'm with cue ball," Bogota said motioning to Frank.

"Not happening," Sledgehammers said.

Bogota took a step back and eyed the huge black man.

"You ain't dressed properly" he said, angling his gaze at Bogota and I and pointing toward the exit. "But if there is a problem?"

Sledgehammers seemed a bit light in the brains department, and Bogota's appearance was short-circuiting his reason.

"No. Not necessary," Bogota said.

TURNED AROUND BEFORE we left, and Frank was settling into a chair and pulling a brown paper bag from his gym bag and exchanging the money inside for colored chips. He had that look on him again, the one from the apple field, that demon monkey was on him, and fixed him like a stanchion. Before the game began, a line of people stopped by the table to shake hands with Frank.

Bogota and I left the back room and took two seats at the bar.

"Drink?" Bogota asked me.

"Bourbon," I said.

"Oh, yeah?" he said. "Which one?"

"The brown one," I said.

"Not yet. I don't think so. Give him a coke," he said to the barmaid, and he looked at me and smiled. "And put some rum in it."

Bogota was demure in the light. He was actually pretty in a sense. I wondered what he looked like before the surgery. The femininity and beauty of his cheeks and hair contradicted the muscled arms and shoulders. He was a mystery in every sense of the world that I know. Yet there was an inescapable draw toward that mystery and the veneer of those gorgeous features that cloaked him, shielding him from questions. Frank said he was a plumber. A plumber was a person that was invited into a home to fix a toilet, to clean up the shit, to probe and fix the works. I could only imagine the disturbed resistance in blue-collar New Jersey homes when a customer opened the door to find this monstrosity.

The life of defending Frank seemed an awfully risky business, considering the investment he had made in his new nose, his cheek bones, his ballooned lips. Yet he was willing to put himself in the line of fire. What answers did he receive when he stared at that beautiful face in the mirror? What was it about Frank that would get him out of bed in the middle of the night to borrow money for an all-night poker game?

"You 21?" the bartender asked and didn't wait for an answer. She turned to fix the drinks.

"And for you?" she asked Bogota.

"Coffee. Black. If you've got it. If it isn't mud."

"Rum is not good," I said.

"Too many Jamaicans?" he asked. "Yup. I've heard that bull-shit too."

"Are you a bourbon man?" I asked.

"No. I'm a coffee man, now."

The rum was sweet, liquid sugar, and I abandoned all of Frank's advice and sipped away at it. The rum brought a hot fluid rush. Maybe Frank was lying about rum. Maybe even about gin. Maybe gin was some sort of briar patch.

"Can I have a gin next?"

"No way," Bogota said. "His theories on liquor are questionable, at best. But the part about gin, I agree unequivocally."

"How do you know?"

"I was a gin drinker."

The clock was the laggard, forever settling on two A.M., and refusing to lift its hands.

"I wish that Frank would just give me a break with this shit."

"Why did you become a plumber?" I asked.

"I fix the shit."

Behind the bar, the rows of liquor were doubled in a large mirror. Bogota and I looked at ourselves and each other, and the reflection allowed us to observe the room. Above the bar were cryptic messages on uneven pieces of wood. "The Strangest life I've ever known." "It's only a good day when I get to kill." "Situation Normal – All Fucked Up" It was some kind of bullshit army humor, but these ominous messages had an undercurrent of hatred, a warning. Above one of the pool tables in the back, there was a plaque dedicated to some shmuck named "Fat Cat," and below were the words "Abandon all hope all ye who enter here."

Bogota treated me to his profile when he looked toward the back of the room.

Joan Crawford? Maybe. Without the eyebrows.

It was an hour and a half later when Frank took a break from the game. Across the pool tables, I could see the back room. Frank exited the room, and began to beat on his chest, which further agitated the other players. I could still see that look in his eyes for another stake. A junkie. I remembered the same demon eye fixed on Will after a good night of Jameson and beer. Frank was that same addict, spiking a vein with wagers. He had the monkey, Will had said. I could see that stranglehold, his spirit and body snatched away, all the willpower devoured and digested, leaving the scrapped and gouged out carcass and soulless specter of the man. Bogota and I would wait for that soul to return to his body, to see if it brought back anything interesting. We would see if it returned at all.

"How goes?" Bogota asked Frank.

"I'd say it goes the way of all flesh."

"For real, Frank. Goddamnit. How goes?"

"I'm up."

"How long?" Bogota asked.

I'm guessing that this is not the first time they have had this discussion.

"I can close in about an hour and a half."

"You still have the 20k?"

"We are way past that."

"I'm worried, Frank."

"Don't be."

Frank took two quick shots of bourbon. He looked to my drink and looked at Bogota. He picked up the glass, sniffed the contents, and took a sip.

"What did I say about rum? Get rid of this," he said to the bartender, pushing the glass. "Give him a beer if he needs anything else. Don't you know rum was almost the collapse of civilized men?"

"You're civilized?" Bogota asked.

He gave Bogota a very stern look and then ran some lip balm over his mouth. A woman in cowboy boots and a tight sweater walked by the bar. "Holy shit, did you see the balloons on her?" he said, forgetting the rum and coke. "My lord, she certainly wouldn't drown," he said marching off and not bothering to wait for us to agree.

Sledgehammers took up sentry again, Frank took his seat back at the table, and the game began again. Bogota flipped his hair and motioned for more coffee.

"Can I ask you something?" I asked.

Bogota let out a long and powerful sigh.

"Once again with the great inquisitor. Ask your questions, and then we are done. Fair enough?"

I reached my hand to him to seal the deal.

"I don't shake hands," he said. "No offense. Now make it good. Anything you like, just no more after this. Is that fair?"

"I really don't have to ask."

"Fair?"

"Fair," I said.

"How do you know Frank?"

He paused for so long that I wasn't sure that he was intending to answer any of my questions.

"I used to work for his father."

"As a plumber?"

"Yeah. Something like that."

"My grandfather?"

"Yeah," he says again in the same exact tone. "Something like that."

OUTSIDE OF FIN'S, Bogota warmed his hands by blowing air into his palms. He said that Frank, "His Royal Pain in the Ass," was probably going to be a while, so we may as well get the hell out of that stink and go find a bite to eat.

"But it's three o'clock in the morning," I said.

"Yes, but Atlantic City is the Night of the Living Dead."

We walked along the clammy street next to the boardwalk. Bogota was right, the streets were still busy with strange looking characters. We walked for a bit, back near to the casino again, and I was starting to feel hungry. Nearby, a bakery had started the morning shift, and the delicious smell of hot bread tickled the air.

I thought about the grandfather that I never met. I never found it odd that grandparents were not part of my world. Linda's story, I already knew. Her mother and father had met during the war and had both died young within a year of one another, long before I was a thought. She didn't talk about them much. At least I could verify their existence with dusty old black and white photos on the mantel and a wedding album with a cracked, faded cover.

I asked Will about his father and mother once, and he told me that his father had died when he was younger. We didn't make much of it afterwards. That was his stalwart approach to family history. It was hard to imagine that Will was ever raised by anyone, or that any part of his reality was not steeped in adulthood. On the long nights when the summer storms would come and he was drunk, he would sometimes mention his father, and talk about what an "asshole" he was. It was as if he excused his own behavior by calling up the worst of his father. When he did mention him, he called him "The Funkie." From what I could make out from his explanation, it was a code word for calling him "The Fuck." He owned one picture of him but never showed it to me. I never thought much of it. At least I knew that Will was an actual human, and that he hadn't been forged in an iron mill in Paterson, NJ.

The generational life of Seton Prep didn't figure into my life. They made a big deal of Legacy Night, a celebration for the alumni who were related to the graduating seniors, a steak dinner in the main hall in Webster, where the bony codgers lined up against the wall with their false teeth and frayed school jackets, Chaz Anderson with facsimiles of more Andersons, balder, rounder, older projections of himself, waddling about the stage and sharing the secret handshake. I didn't need to represent on Legacy night. I was fresh out of grandparents and bequests. I didn't need to pack the bleachers on graduation day with a sea of white-haired replicas. I didn't need their faux history. I had Uncle George (armed with a flask of Jack Daniels) and Aunt Margaret who would probably show up. I had another slew of aunts who were Linda's sisters, and I had the scattered remains of Will's relatives we knew from floating in and out of our holidays. I had cousins, somewhere. But no grandparents. Linda and Will were enough. Now I had Frank too. And maybe Bogota. If I could find out anything about him.

"So, what was your job?"

"I fixed things. I already told you this."

He flashed that runway model look at me and gave a wink. I guessed that the Q & A had ended. We walked back toward the ocean; the salty whips of air stung our faces. Bogota was leading at a determined pace. The false pillars of Caesar's Casino rose from the boardwalk, the statues of Roman Gods hovering like sentries. We rode a bank of escalators down into the pit of cackling slot machines and flashing lights. Bogota changed a hundred dollars for ten rolls of quarters and slouched his huge mass in front of one of the machines. He fixated on the lights without moving and then finally began to slot the coins. Each attempt was a failure.

His giant mass and strange features commanded the room. He chose a slot machine that was backed into a corner, far away from questioning eyes.

"There was a black dog that we saw on the street every day for a week," Bogota said.

A waitress came over to offer us a drink. Bogota sent her away. He fed the machine more coins and hit three cherries for a six-point payoff. He left the coins in the tray and spun the machine again. Beyond the rows of slot machines, the blackjack tables were crowded with bodies even for this time of night.

"Money was pouring into this town at that time. The Governor gave the go-ahead, and buildings were getting knocked down all over AC and put up at breakneck speed. The whole place was getting a facelift," he said and laughed to himself.

The lights of the slot machine flickered, and a melodic invitation followed whenever it became idle for too long. He dumped a few more coins and had a minor success, three bells for a payoff of twenty coins.

"We had a gut job on Pacific, an old, abandoned warehouse, and the boss had me looking after the demo crew. Not too far from where we are now. The city was going to demolish the building anyway, but the boss wanted to get all the scrap copper from the walls."

Bogota went on a losing streak, but he kept pumping the machine.

"That dog was there every day, ugly looking thing, poking around for food. No matter how much we shooed it away, it still came back. Some of the Mexican laborers were nasty and they would give it a good kick. But, still he just kept coming back."

The waitress was making her rounds again. I flagged her down and asked her for a drink. Bogota told her not to serve me. "Enough for tonight with that shit. What are you suddenly an alcoholic?" he said to me and then continued. "It was a stinking ugly city," Bogota said. "But in the mornings, before we started, I would go to the top of the buildings and watch those sunrises. You just can't ruin a sunrise. And, every morning, I would hear that dog barking."

He stopped playing again and folded his hands into his lap.

"Then one day, he was just dead on the sidewalk, stiff, on his back with his legs in the air."

The machine howled at him.

"He still had a collar on and tags, so he had to have belonged to someone. But no one bothered to collect him. One morning there was a good chunk of the shoulder gone, chewed off, and some birds had pecked out its guts. Still, they just left him there."

A crowd of frat boys passed by the slot machines followed by girls in evening dresses. One of the boys looked over his shoulder. "Nice fucking face!" Then they hurried off.

Luckily for him, Bogota just ignored him. "He just laid there." He scanned the casino floor. "The day laborers would toss rocks to see who could hit him from the roof. Perro muerto, Pobre Perro, and then finally Perro Negro, they called him. They would bet on just about anything. So, they took action on how long he would be there. Perro Negro was there for a week. One day, I picked him up. He stunk like hell, and his left eye was missing. The dumpster pick-up was at noon, so I tossed him on top. He didn't weigh much. Most of him was gone. They said that I fixed the game. They started calling me Perro Negro because you didn't want to see me coming."

I could see that dead dog, and its rotted guts, dead eyes, forgotten, swollen with maggots. The world just not giving a good goddamn about any of it. That was the worst part.

"I bet one of those Mexican cunts put a bullet in him, and nobody gave a damn enough to pick him up off of the sidewalk."

He collected his winnings and changed them back into dollars. "Get it. I fix shit when it needs fixing."

THE TRUNK SLAMMED and a hard knock at the door startled Bogota and I from sleep and into a dizzying, blinding sunlight. Bogota was behind the wheel. He had kept watch most of the night, but I suppose we feel asleep. I remembered that the car was on, but now the engine was silent, and the inside was freezing. Frank was red-eyed, and his face was swollen from no sleep. He jumped into the passenger seat.

"Start the car. Go!"

Bogota jumped from his seat. He began to reach for the duffel bag in the back, but instead he started the car and peeled out of the driveway.

"What the hell happened?" He was awake now and racing down the side streets.

Frank just smiled at him.

"You're an asshole," he said. He slowed the Chevy to a normal pace. "Gonna give me a fucking heart attack one of these days."

"Just crying wolf," Frank said.

"So, how bad is it?" Bogota asked. "So how much did you lose?"

"Who says that I lost?"

The Chevy sped out of town, eased back onto the highway, and rattled back through the swampy, southern New Jersey landscape.

"Did you two have a nice date?" he asked Bogota

"I know that I could find better things to do then this," he said. He was clearly mad. "And I'm sure that he could do the same," he threw a thumb back towards me.

I tried to sleep again, but it was useless. We stopped at a diner. The place was empty except for a briny waitress with a lazy eye who looked as though she was winking all the time. She was clearly irritated by our presence. Frank tried to coax her into making three margaritas. She refused. He produced another twenty for her, and she returned with the drinks.

"Is he old enough?" she asked.

"Old enough for what?"

"To drink alcohol!"

"I'm the only one that is drinking," Frank said. He sucked them down instantly. "Another round, please."

"One more?"

"No. Another round," Frank said, using his forefinger to make a circle, indicating that he wanted a full round of everything that he ordered before. "And a beer."

"Frank, what happened back there?" Bogota asked.

"Nothing I can't handle."

"This is insane, man. You got this kid here, and you spend all goddamn night at the table. I thought this was supposed to be a little trip."

"It just happened."

"Like it always just happens."

Frank reached into his belt and pulled out several bundles of hundred-dollar bills and laid them on the table. Next, he removed a gold Rolex watch and held it up to the light. He reached over, grabbed Bogota's wrist and clipped the watch onto his forearm.

"Looks good. What do you think?"

Bogota held up his arm and laughed. "Never a dull moment, Frank."

Frank separated two piles of the bills into thousand-dollar stacks. I looked around the diner wondering if anyone would come in and see the insane amount of cash that was on the table.

"So, you won?" Bogota asks.

"Yes. I whooped their ass in five card stud. You shoulda seen me. Couldn't lose."

"That scares me more than anything."

The winking, irritated waitress returned with three more margaritas that were almost clear from the amount of tequila that she had put in them. I'm sure her greatest fear was coming to fruition. She had to wait on a sniffling, red-eyed, drunken nut job who drank tequila at six in the morning, a gigantic woman/man, and a kid who was too confused and nervous to make up his mind about the menu. On Thanksgiving morning no less. The look on her face changed when she saw the money on the table. Frank peeled off a hundred-dollar bill and handed it to her.

Her irritation was gone. She looked as though she would suddenly cry.

"Just keep them coming, sweetheart," Frank said.

Bogota stared at his watch. The waitress left us, and I could see her near the end of the long counter holding up the hundred-dollar bill into the light. I noticed a pay phone and I thought of Will and Linda. We had been gone for a full day, and it felt like a hundred years.

Frank collected the money into neat piles again and stuffed the bills into his belt.

"You are un-fucking-believable," Bogota said.

Bogota kept his sunglasses on. He watched the parking lot. We shared in Frank's victory. The light reflected from the golden watch. I wondered why we needed the dramatic escape if he'd actually won. I was through with trying to figure out Frank.

Bogota finally ordered a coffee. I had pancakes.

I don't think that Frank was a big fan of having anyone drive the Chevy, so he went off to the bathroom and washed out his eyes. I could hear him as he voided all the snot from his nose. He was ready to take the helm once again, even though he was blasted from six margaritas and no food. Bogota was more than happy to turn over the reins, maybe even hopeful that Frank might drive us all over the side of cliff and he could be done with this whole debacle. Of course, there was time for one beer for Frank before we left.

Back on the road, the lanes narrowed as we crossed over a bridge. We were almost halted completely by a herd of cyclists pedaling out of New Jersey.

"What in the fuck are these imbeciles doing, riding bikes on Thanksgiving morning? God, I hate cyclists. There is far too much preparation in the attire. A man needs to exercise like a man, not a fashion show."

"'No contraries hold more antipathy than I and such a knave,'" Bogota whispered, looking at Frank.

"Hangovers are only hangovers if you choose to sleep. I choose to marshal the parade. Someone has to."

"You are drunk then?"

"I didn't say that."

"So, you are hungover then?"

"I didn't say that either."

Bogota let the conversation end.

"Brogan, open your door."

"Why am I opening the door?" I asked.

"Because you don't want to walk back to Jersey." Frank said.

I was behind the passenger seat in the Chevy. I unlocked the door, gripped the handle, and opened the door slightly.

"All the way!" Frank yelled.

Frank slowed the Chevy to a crawl and aimed the car toward the riders. One of the cyclists was pedaling hard. When he saw us, he jerked his handlebars away and almost took out the whole crew. One of the other characters pedaled toward us shaking his fist. He didn't look that threatening in his neon green and pink get-up.

"You can shut the door now, Brogan."

I could hear the group shouting "fuck you" and "assholes." Frank revved up the engine and we shot down the road. For once, the music was off. Bogota smirked, then snickered, then began to laugh. Frank laughed with him. I couldn't believe what I was hearing. The laughter was breaking glass and dangerous. I wondered if someone should be calling an ambulance, and I was wondering why these lunatics were laughing. This was not funny.

WE STOPPED DRIVING only when we needed gas. Frank would hustle off to the pay phones with his quarters and his notebook. Bogota would silently watch for his return. After the second stop Bogota returned from the convenience store at the gas station and brought me a toothbrush and toothpaste, a bar of soap, and some aspirin. He told me to go and get cleaned up. And, to take off that ridiculous looking suit. My head hurt terribly from the mix of booze from Fin's. I cleaned up in the gas station restroom.

When I returned to the Chevy, Bogota was trimming his nails and sitting on the hood.

"You got a girlfriend?" he asked me.

"No."

"Why not?"

"Do you?"

Bogota laughed at this. He took off his jacket, got down on the pavement, and began doing pushups. After twenty or so, he stopped and leaned on his elbow and looked at me. He motioned me to join him. I tried to keep up. When I couldn't do anymore, he stood up and grabbed me by the back of my shirt and lifted me up and down until I could no longer feel my arms and then I collapsed.

"I did have a girl. She made off with the town asshole," I said.

"Did you bust him in the chops?"

"He's pretty tough."

"She ain't worth it," Bogota said. "I still think that you should have cracked him anyway."

"I'm not so good at that sort of thing."

"Yes. I've heard."

I told more of the story to Bogota about Andrea and Laforte. It was better than asking him questions, but, after a while, I was certain that I was grating on his nerves. He listened to the end.

"What can I tell you?" he said.

"Thanks. That helps me," I said with a bit of sarcasm.

"Let's see."

"Let's see about what?"

"We are going to give her a call."

"Now? Are you serious? Wait!"

He was already walking across the parking lot.

"I'm going to make this very simple for you," he said, and he took two steps back. He looked me directly in the eyes and mouthed the words without speaking. I didn't know what he wanted me to do. He tried it again. I still didn't get it. I stared at him.

"Are you retarded?" he finally said.

"No."

"Good. We have that figured out then. Maybe I wasn't clear. When I mouth the words you say them back to me. You repeat it. Got It?"

"Yes."

He stepped back again. As always, I was distracted by his perfectly formed lips. They were glossy perimeters that framed flawless white teeth. It took all of my concentration, but I read his lips and I fed back his words to him.

"I'm Brogan," I said, sounding out his words, and repeating them back to him. "And I may be an idiot."

I stopped when I realized what he was saying. "That's not funny," I said.

"No. It's not, but at least I know that now you are not brain damaged. Let's give this a try. Remember, only say *what I say*."

He fished some coins from his pocket and dropped them in the slot. "Dial," he said.

While I typed the familiar numbers, he directed me. "Follow my directions precisely. I'm going to look directly at you while you are talking to her, and I am going to whisper what I want you to say to her. Let me hear what she is saying, and then I want you to say exactly what I say. Got it?"

"Hello," came the voice of Andrea's mother already flush with alcohol in the early morning. I was frustrated that it wasn't Andrea who picked up. I never liked her mother that much. In our few interactions when she was sober, she was a miserable wreck in a depressing pink robe and a cloud of cigarette smoke. More often than not she was loaded, which gave her a twinge of an English accent from God knows where. She would smoke her cigarettes from a holder. When she would see me, she would sneer over her turned up nose. I'm pretty sure she hated my guts.

When she answered the phone, I could hear the pseudo-English accent even over the clamor of heavy traffic. I recognized the bubbling noise of a glass being filled. I froze and handed Bogota the phone.

"Ah…Hello," Bogota said. "This is Reginald. Is Andrea home?"

"Reginald? Who?"

He covered the receiver and whispered to me, "This woman is already aggravating the piss out of me, and she only said two words. Is she English?"

"Hello!" The voice made us both twinge. "Who are you?"

"I'm Reginald, the stock trader from the New York Mercantile Exchange," he said.

She changed her tune. "Reginald," she said in a purring voice. In my mind, I imagine giving her healthy rump a good punt.

"My goodness. However did you meet?" she said, sounding like the duchess of Windsor.

"At the coffee shop," Bogota said.

"Quick Bite!"

"Where else?" he said matter of fact. "I'm sorry to cut you short, but I have to catch a plane to Monte Carlo to meet a client."

"Good God!" she screamed, recovering her New Jersey accent for a moment.

Bogota covered the phone receiver. "Is this woman insane?"

I shrugged my shoulders in a way that suggested "perhaps."

"I'll get her right away!" She sounded like she was about to have a coronary right on the spot. Bogota handed me back the phone.

"What? I don't know," I heard Andrea saying to her mother and then I heard her voice in the receiver. "Reginald? Who is this?" She sounded genuinely confused.

"Hey Andrea, it's me. Don't hang up."

Bogota stood a foot away from me and pressed his fingers to his lips, indicating for me to shush. He mouthed the words to me, "Just say what I say."

"Just say what I say," I said. He rolled his eyes at this, bent his head and just nodded in frustration. He shushed me. I nodded.

"Brogan, you have to be kidding me. How's life on Mars?"

"Brogan! What does he want?" I heard her mother say in the background.

"Mother, please be quiet," she said.

I was about to say something when Bogota hissed at me to shut up. "Let her talk."

"I just…"

Bogota shoved me. He mouthed the words and I repeated them, not really absorbing what he was saying, but obeying.

"It's just that I see you all the time and it seems as if," Bogota paused to think, and I pumped my hand at him. He smiled and continued. 'It seems as though the time in between seeing you is as if I have slept a thousand years and now, I am awake."

I stopped, punched him on the shoulder, and covered the phone. "It's too much!"

"Shut up," he said and motioned for me to continue. He was about to begin mouthing words again, but then he stopped. He no longer whispered. "Don't ever touch me again."

Andrea was becoming impatient. "Hello? Who is talking in the back?"

"Yours is a face that I have known before birth." I was turning eighteen shades of red and swore that I would murder him.

"You are the silent streets before dawn, the waking moment, a breath of sunlight in golden-pearled birdsong. Of wistful afternoons, and windswept meadow grass, the paradise scent of autumn apple paths."

I cringed. I waited for the inevitable laughter and the phone to come slamming down.

"Wow," was all that she said.

Bogota continued, and I said his words. "I'm with my uncle. I will be back soon. I hope (I added). I would like to take you out sometime. I've always felt that way about you. If you don't want to go out with me, I understand. But I wanted you to know how I felt. I just think, as strange as it sounds, that I would like to know you for the rest of my life."

The line was silent with an exhausting long pause. She sighed into the phone. I heard a click and the dial tone.

"She hung up," I said. "How the hell did you just make all of that up?"

"What did I tell you about all of the questions?"

BOGOTA WALKED TO the other end of the line of phones where Frank was jabbering away. Bogota and I stood on either side of him.

"Somewhere in the neighborhood of 50k," Frank said. When he saw Bogota, he cupped his hand over the receiver and waved us away.

"Again, with the 50k!" Bogota said.

Frank held the phone down and pointed toward the car.

"We have other business," Bogota said to me. He picked up that same insane pace which forced me to almost jog to keep up with him.

"Oh?"

"This Andrea, she good looking?"

"Absolutely."

"And the Laforte guy keeps getting in the way?"

"Most of the time."

"Dump her. Get rid of her."

"I have to be dating her to be able to get rid of her."

"Don't bother with her is what I'm saying. Why are you wasting your time?"

"I don't have a choice."

He stopped and thought about this and nodded his head.

"Understood. Fine. Do what you like. But I have business with you. From what Frank says, you can't fight worth a shit."

I didn't say anything. I had already proven that twice over lately. Once, with Chaz Anderson, and once with the two knuckleheads from the convenience store.

"And I saw that poor excuse for a punch that you have."

Bogota took off his jacket, exposing his massive arms.

"Listen, you're not that big and you definitely don't look too scary. Truth be told, I still think this Laforte kid needs a good crack. So, you are going to learn the basics, at least."

"Now?"

"We have time to kill," he said, throwing a thumb back in Frank's direction. "And besides, Frank insists."

"He does?"

"OK, show me your fighting stance."

"I don't have one."

Bogota got into his fighting stance and then dropped his hands in frustration. "Didn't Will show you any of this?"

"No."

"Are you a righty or lefty?"

I shrugged.

"Jesus H.! Which hand do you write with? How do you hold a hockey stick?"

I shrugged again.

"Which hand do you jerk off with?"

I held up my right.

"Finally. All right, then. Put your left foot forward." He put his left in front, drawing back his right foot and crouching into a fighter's stance. He eliminated all targets and scrunched into a powerful tank with two cannons poised strategically to strike, while simultaneously defending his chin and temple.

"This is a jab." He shot a straight punch, snapped it back with amazing speed for his size. He tucked his chin under his enormous shoulder. "I lead with my left, so always walk away from right.

Never walk into my power hand, or you're going to get a lesson in counting ceiling tiles. Now, show me your stance."

I put my hands up. He took a step back, eyed me, and delivered a quick slap off the side of my temple. I dropped my hands.

"Dammit! That hurt."

"Shut up. Keep your hands up. Good. Now try another jab."

I snapped another good solid jab. He moved in a circular path, and I followed and stayed away from his power hand. I popped out two more good jabs, but it was awkward.

"Relax. You look like a monkey fucking a football. It's not like that. See this as a dance, be fluid and loose."

He did move in a fluid and liquid dance that seemed almost impossible for his size. His motions were a river, legs and arms flowing in and out in a dangerous dance.

It's hard to conjure someone you want to hit when you just don't have that much anger. I thought of Rich Laforte and the two idiots who roughed me up at the convenience store just hours ago. But their images were already fading. Whatever offense they had given me was losing strength. I didn't have the ability to hold a grudge. Bogota was different. He smoldered. He hummed like a tractor-trailer engine. Hate was his bride. The technicalities of boxing were a functional tool for him, a necessity, and a constant pair of guns in a ready holster.

Bogota showed me the mechanics of the jab, then a hook, then an uppercut, and finally, his favorite, the right cross. "That's your dandy," he said. "A straight right to the chin will shut any engine down." Then he showed me how to put the punches together into combinations while using his mammoth open palms for boxing mitts. He gave the combinations numbers one through six and called them out. I fumbled in the beginning but then got the rhythm and the right mix of punches. It was even fun for a few rounds, but it made the shoulders burn. I lowered my hands and suddenly caught a powerful smack to the side of the head. The sting was enormous and painful, but more so humiliating.

"This isn't about being smart. This isn't a valedictorian thing, Brogan, this is liquid and water, a river, a wind. If you're mad, then you've lost."

I took a step back, feigning pain. I was mad. I saw Chaz Anderson. I launched a combination at Bogota. He dipped and weaved with such grace, then clipped me with another solid slap on the other side of my head.

"Keep your hands up, Goddamnit! Always protect yourself!"

"This is my first time," I said. I could feel the tears of humiliation welling in my eyes.

"Oh, maybe your opponent should ask you first how many fights you've had. I'll tell you this right now! Don't even think about crying!"

But I did begin to cry. I was humiliated. I was definitely pissed. I hated the tears more than anything. They far outweighed any pain that I may have felt.

I went at him. I took a misstep. The procedure didn't seem quite right. The fluid motion and ease of before somehow went against the grain. In the flurry of elbows and fists and legs, I went right most certainly when I should have gone left. I felt a thud, saw a flash of white, passed into a dreamy state, and soon tasted the chalky asphalt. For the second time.

When I came to, Bogota was putting his jacket back on and shaking his head at Frank. "Hopeless."

Frank had one foot on the bumper of the Chevy, watching the match. "Got to learn to keep your hands up, boy."

MONEY," FRANK SAID, "It's the fool's carrot and the devil's ensemble."

The hours on the road were undecided on dreams or reality. In Delaware, the lonely Route Thirteen was a repetitive tale of soy and corn fields and solitary farmhouses plopped down in the middle of the grain like tossed white hats.

I had trouble sleeping the year that Dan passed away. Most of my dreams became nightmares. In one of the worst, Dan and I rode in a limousine. Dan was sitting next to me in his shit-stained pants, and his bloated, unnatural face. He kept trying to explain the importance of the clitoris.

On top of that, with Linda gone and Will drinking most of the time, I learned to become a light sleeper anyway. Even after their return, I would awaken in the early morning hours with a start, knowing that it would be some time until I could sleep again. Out of the habit of looking after Will, I would walk through the house, checking the windows and the doors, making sure that cigarettes were not burning. Linda had put a stop to all smoking in the house anyway, but still, I would search. It was during one of those late-night watches that I found myself looking at a framed black and white photo of Will as a teenager. He was outside of a place called Costello's, a boxing gym in Paterson, with his face pitched up in a smug snarl. He was shirtless, with boxing gloves tied around his neck

For his own reasons, Will had never taught me the basics, and it was evident in my recent string of defeats. He had always tried to keep me off the road he had taken. I knew that he had been in and out of jail quite a bit as a kid. Furthermore, Linda was adamant that I follow a different route in all respects. Still, it seemed a rudimentary skill that I could have used. And, not to mention, he was good at it.

When we stopped, Bogota insisted on rehearsing the combinations. I snapped out more jabs, stabbing at the empty space, dancing away from his power hand, slipping the sweeps of counterpunches above my head, being more quicksand than liquid, but showing some improvement. He taught me the overhand right and insisted that I at least learn one good punch. When I didn't get it right, Bogota reminded me with a good tap dance on my head. Always protect yourself.

Frank watched the progress, offering his own advice and commentary. "Slip beneath his jab. If you make him miss, then make him pay." That advice made sense. I noticed that sometimes Bogota threw a lazy jab, testing the air. I waited. I timed it. I moved fluidly, dipped, stepped in. Bogota threw a jab, and I slipped beneath his huge arm and gave him a good tap to the ribs.

"Whoah!" Frank yelled. "Not bad."

Bogota stopped immediately and looked at Frank and then me. Our lesson was done. He put on his jacket and his dark sunglasses and walked away.

"What was that all about?" I asked.

"Pay it no mind," Frank said. "He just doesn't like people touching him."

"I wonder about that, Frank," I said. "Is he?"

"Is he what?"

"You know my question."

"Why don't you ask him that?"

"Yeah, right."

"Listen, Brogan. Every man has his own ice cream. Let them choose their own flavors. Oh, and be proud of yourself, there aren't too many people that ever got a shot in on him." He jumped down from the car hood. "And kept their teeth afterwards."

I smiled and snapped out a few practice swings using the window of the Chevy to shadowbox. Bogota was in front of the car, fixing his hair, and reapplying his makeup.

"Be careful," Frank said walking away. "If you hit the car, I may have to beat you into a coma."

We were back on the road and by early afternoon we were well into North Carolina. The road was knotted with holiday travelers. Frank swore up and down. We exited and drove past a high school. The basketball courts were filled with a group of kids around my own age. It was Thanksgiving afternoon, but the weather was fair. It was getting warmer the further we drove south. They wore t-shirts and shorts.

Earlier, I had changed back into the only clothes that I had, jeans, a Sex Pistols t-shirt and combat boots.

"This one should be fine," Frank said to Bogota.

He pulled the car into the empty parking lot.

"Basketball is a lesson on individuality." Frank slipped off the sweat-stained flowery shirt from the night before and put on a t-shirt. He still hadn't slept, and I could tell the buzz of the margaritas had worn off. He was a bit ornery. "Although, you are part of a team, you are also an island out there. You need to learn to adjust on the fly. To look for open space. To make something happen that you didn't think of before. To let the momentum of the competition take you somewhere you didn't anticipate going."

Frank may have been speaking Chinese for as much as I could understand what he was talking about.

"What's this nonsense about the 50k?" Bogota asked.

"I got this thing going," Frank said.

"You're digging your own grave, Frank," Bogota said. "Let's just take the rest of this trip and forget about that bullshit. Take the kid to goddamn Disneyland. Do something for him."

"I am doing something for him. I'm giving him an education."

Bogota got out of the car and spat on the ground.

"Were heading south," Frank said. He was still distracted by the basketball game.

Bogota left and was walking around the empty field.

Frank was watching Bogota. "Most people are pricks," he said to me. "You're gonna learn that."

"I've known a few," I said.

Bogota was getting a lot of attention from the group of basketball players. They wouldn't dare say anything to him. He walked over to the court and began a conversation with one of the boys on the sidelines. The kid didn't look much older than me. He had bad acne and a slick of unkempt and shiny black hair, but most noticeably, he had a big potbelly.

"You start with that huge circle of people in your life," Frank said, ignoring my response. "And you go from there: your family, your friends, people you work with, high school, college (if you go that route), that guy down at the grocery store. Day after day they pile up. You think they are all special to you. After a while, you begin to whittle them down. They are just waves of energy. You find that you are not on the same frequency anymore. One by one they dissipate, like radio waves that disappear into space. They don't mean as much to you anymore. Then you find yourself down to just a small group you share your life with. Then, it's just a few you tell your secrets to." He stops and thinks. "And there is one you tell just about everything." Outside, Bogota bummed a cigarette from one of the players on the sideline, and Frank followed his movements. "There's just that one person, one wave that you connect with. One who actually knows you."

Bogota's enormous frame blocked out the sun, and he cast a large shadow on the ground.

"A friend in need is a friend indeed," Frank said.

"What does that even mean?" I asked.

"It means if a snake bit you on the ass, would your friend be enough of a friend to suck the poison out?" Frank said.

Bogota finished the cigarette. I thought that he had quit smoking. He walked back to the car. "Looks like we're good to go."

"You any good at basketball?" Frank asked.

"No," I said.

"Good. We are going to play."

"Now? Against who?"

"Them," Frank said. Pointing to the basketball courts. The scatter of boys on the court were about two years older than me, but that made all the difference. They were taller and more fit. They moved with a sense of both grace and determination, angling into spin moves and driving to the basket. They didn't have the lean street look of most of my New Jersey friends. They were farm fed. About a cow a day by the size of them. Three of them sectioned off from the others and began to take practice shots together. One of them was Potbelly. He seemed to lead the team. He called plays and then circled around, passing the ball and then shooting. The other two boys were definitely brothers. They had long shaggy blond hair and the only way that they were distinguishable, was the different concert t-shirts that they wore. One was of Metallica and the other Slayer.

"Great," I said with a bit of sarcasm.

Frank, Bogota, and I were all dressed in jeans and boots. Perfect athletic gear. Frank and Bogota moved onto the court. One of the boys threw the basketball to Bogota. He palmed the orange ball in his enormous hands like he was holding a marble. He was much taller than everyone. He took a shot with one hand, made the basket, and then walked off toward the sidelines. He was clearly uninterested.

We took a few practice shots. Frank was a pretty good shot. He landed most of his free throws and a couple of shots from odd angles. He threw the ball to me. I missed every shot. Bogota came back, and we separated into two sides. We took free throw shots to see who would have possession first. Frank matched Potbelly for two shots and then missed on the third.

We would start on defense. Frank pointed for me to cover Potbelly. Potbelly threw the ball at me, and I held on to it, not sure why he would give me the ball if we were on offense.

"Check the ball."

I looked at Frank.

"Check the ball," Frank said.

"I don't know what that means."

"Give him back the ball and say check."

"Check," I said. I threw him back the ball. He quickly threw a pass to the boy that Frank was covering, who threw another pass, and then they scored right away. They got the ball back again.

"Check," Potbelly said. He smiled, then instead of passing me the ball, he intentionally bounced the ball off of my forehead. I was confused and angry. "Got the gist of it now?" He took the rebound off of my head, backed up two paces, and sunk a long jump shot.

"Two – zip," he said.

"Cut the shit," Frank said to Potbelly.

"What the hell was that?" I asked.

"What?" Potbelly said smugly. "Check!"

I put my hands up in time to catch the ball before it ricocheted off my forehead again. These southern boys were fast. Even Potbelly, who was carrying a bit of luggage in the front, faked me out with a head nod and quickly drove to the basket. Bogota didn't move. Frank was actually smoking a cigarette. They gave each other high fives, and pats on the ass.

"How about a little defense!" Frank said to Bogota.

"How about covering the pick!" Bogota said to Frank.

The game was determined by whichever team scored twenty-one first. Metallica and Slayer were amazingly agile for their size. I mostly covered Potbelly, but in the action, I was forced to cover the brothers as well. We eventually got the ball and Bogota and Frank combined for a few points. It was clear that they knew one another's movements. The simple fact was that if you were able to get the ball to Bogota, he was so tall that you would have to climb up his back to stop him from scoring. I checked the ball again, and when it was returned to me, I tried to take a shot, but Potbelly leapt up and slammed the ball back at me and nearly to the other basket.

"Goddamnit Brogan, you could read that play from New Jersey! Think! Improvise! Be creative!"

The three boys laughed and bumped chests with one another. The crowd was growing around us, and they shouted with hoots and catcalls.

"Tighten up, Brogan!" Bogota yelled.

Bogota was checking the ball now. He gave me a quick pass. I looked to pass again to Frank. I never saw Potbelly coming. He flattened me onto my back with an elbow to the chest. He grabbed the ball, passed it to his teammate to get it back on sides. They scored again.

"Game point," he said.

"That's not fair," I said.

"Not fair," Potbelly mimicked me, and the rest of the team laughed. "You don't even know what a 'check' is."

"That's a blatant penalty."

"It's a called a foul. And that wasn't a foul."

"You cheated."

"Damn boy," he said with his southern accent. "You gonna play ball? Or cry all day?"

"Frank!"

"Get back on defense," Frank said. "Let's go! Get back in the game!"

Potbelly walked purposefully slow back to the foul line. He checked the ball to Bogota and made a quick pass. I had Metallica pretty well covered. I was flailing my arms like an idiot. I anticipated a pass and I rushed to Slayer. Then, suddenly, I was on the ground again, and I had ripped my jeans. Potbelly had purposefully stuck out his leg and tripped me. They scored twenty-one and had won the game.

"That doesn't count," I said getting up quickly. "He tripped me. That's a foul."

"It's called a pick," he said.

"You tripped me on purpose. We get the ball back."

"Game's over," Potbelly said.

"You cheated," I said. "Again."

He walked over, stood about an inch away from my face, then he shoved me onto the ground. I looked at Frank and Bogota. They didn't make a move. Frank folded his arms and waited. "We shouldn't have lost," I said from the ground.

"Looks like it's time to ante up," Frank says.

"Now, that is a blatant *penalty*," Potbelly said.

Potbelly allowed me enough room to get up. Then he shoved me onto the ground again. Bogota and Frank took up strategic positions for observation and referee. I got up quick this time and took a few steps back. "What the hell are you doing?" I felt my legs moving me toward the fight, drawing into a dream. My arms were rubber. My mouth had gone suddenly dry. The crowd of boys gathered around us. Before I knew it, we were walking to the dusty field nearby.

"What is this all about, anyway—" Before I could finish, Potbelly had landed a good, solid shot, missing my nose, but catching me square on the forehead. My knees abandoned me, and I dropped to the ground. The crowd jeered. Bogota looked away, annoyed and frustrated.

"You're in it now, boy," Frank said. "Keep your hands up!"

Potbelly delivered a hard kick and threw a knee into my side. "That's called a combination," he said.

I found my legs and stood up, feeling more confused than anything. Potbelly came at me one more time. I felt an anger that I didn't know existed. I threw a punch wild, which he blocked, and he delivered a straight shot. A sudden flash of white light, and I was back on the ground and checking to make sure that I hadn't lost a tooth. *If you are mad then you have lost.* The ground was becoming a familiar place. Frank and Bogota did not move. The humiliation outweighed the pain.

This was not my world, this isolation and blunt violence. A world that wasn't going to give a good goddamn whether you were ready for it or not. The tears were shameful. For a moment, I thought of Dan. He'd been dead for four years, but he hadn't left me. I remembered him fighting in the Dewey School playground, squaring up to Laforte, anteing up. Laforte had knocked him down three times, but he kept getting up. He kept coming even after the battle was lost. He never looked mad, just determined. I didn't want to fight any more for Frank or Bogota. I would never allow Dan to see me give up.

I got to one knee and spit out the blood. Potbelly was about to put on his jacket, which one of his friends was handing him, but he refused it when he saw me standing again. He walked back over with a confident smirk. His hands were low. He was not ready to protect himself. I noticed that he was squared up to me and not favoring one foot or the other. Since he delivered both times with the right, I figured him for a righty and began to move toward his left. I brought my hands up and protected my chin and temple. He threw a hard right again, but it landed on the crook of my elbow. It still hurt like hell, but this time I was still standing.

I heard Bogota's voice. Combination number two. I let go. I stepped away from his right hand and snapped out the jab that Bogota taught me, pulled it back, and fired again.

There exists an amazing satisfaction to delivering a punch that lands square and precise. The double shot surprised and infuriated Potbelly. He had lost the fluidity now. He had forgotten the dance. He threw another wild one, and this time, I used the number two combination: a double jab and a right cross. It landed beautifully on his nose, and a spray of blood shot onto his t-shirt. He was blinded, and his hands immediately went to his face.

I moved in.

Forgetting the combinations, I felt the blood lust and began to throw wildly at his head. Most of the shots missed, but one landed square on his temple and sent him to the ground.

I got on top of him, and my fists crunched against his face, and his blood covered my hands and shirt. Two older boys from the crowd parted us and said that Potbelly had had enough, and the fight should be over. Frank cheered, and Bogota patted me on the back. He lifted me half on his shoulder and carried me on a victory lap. It didn't feel like victory. My teeth felt loose, and my clothes were a mess of blood and dirt. It was amazing how short a true fist fight lasted. I was still crying.

Potbelly collected himself and began to head toward us. He had removed his shirt, and he was wiping away the blood from his mouth and nose. The same blood was on my hands. I was exhausted and shaking. I couldn't believe that he actually wanted to continue.

"Isn't that enough?" I asked.

He didn't approach me. He walked over to Frank and Bogota, and Bogota handed him a twenty dollar bill.

"Good fight," Potbelly said to me and turned and walked back to the court and started shooting baskets again.

I looked from Frank to Bogota and back at Frank.

"Fuck you both," I said.

"Hey," Frank said. He was surprised by my reaction.

"You needed to learn properly," Bogota said.

"Fuck you," I said again.

Happy Birthday Brogan!

Between life and death, there is a stream, decide which side of the bank is yours, and if you jump in, whether you will follow the current. Oh, also stop running from the girls in the schoolyard and start chasing them. Trust me. You're twelve and the Country is two hundred years old now. Everything is relative.

Love, Frank.

THE BATHROOM WAS empty. I stood by the sink, running cold water, with the pinkish liquid flowing from my mouth and swirling into the drain. I guess that I had a good story now. But I just didn't get Frank and his lessons. In the mirror, I saw a few yellowish and blue bruises collecting on my forehead and cheek. I felt a tooth that was now a bit loose.

I washed my face and when I looked up, I found Bogota and Frank in the mirror. Bogota was leaning against the sinks and picking at his nails. Frank was seated on the ledge and dangling his feet. I wondered about him and Frank, and what Frank said about having one person who truly knows you. I wondered whether Dan was the one person who knew me. Perhaps I was the one person who understood him. I

wonder, if Dan had lived, if there would have been crazy adventures for us, and whether Los Angeles was as amazing as he imagined, and whether we would have dug up the decaying corpse of Jim Morrison, and whether his casket would have been empty.

Bogota placed a painfully ugly yellow T-shirt that he bought in the gas station next to me. I took off the stained one that I was wearing and used it as a towel.

"You can't play basketball worth a shit, but you did damn good," Bogota said.

I dabbed at my mouth and stared at him in the mirror.

"That was a dirty goddamned trick," I said.

Bogota continued to prune himself in the mirror. A dull ache rose in the arm that I used to block the punch.

His voice echoed from the tiled walls. He lit a cigarette.

The cool water felt good. Bogota and Frank also were now wearing yellow t-shirts. They looked ridiculous.

"Sometimes, we need to find ourselves in situations where we can achieve greatness," Frank said.

"So, you purposefully put me in a dangerous situation because of your cockeyed theories?"

"Well, you proved me right."

Frank jumped off the ledge and ambled back out outside. Bogota and I eyed each other in the mirror.

"Don't drop your shoulder when you throw the right cross," Bogota said. "If you'd missed that punch, you were done for."

"But I didn't. Did I?" I snapped.

"Don't get smart with me," he said.

"I don't even know what I'm doing here," I said. In the mirror, my naked chest was white, frail and exposed. "What are you doing here, anyway? Why do you look like that? Why do you protect him? Oh. Wait! That's just a bunch of questions! I can't ask you questions, but you can set up mismatched fist fights for me because you think

I need it. I don't need it. I'm pretty smart, you know. Do you even know what college I'm going to next year?"

"The Massachusetts Institute of Technology Boston, Massachusetts," he said. "Ten percent acceptance rate. Full scholarship. No wonder everyone kisses your ass at that school."

The response was quick and precise.

"Real fucking genius," he said. "I know about the scholarship. I know about the time you had pneumonia, and William, your father, wouldn't leave you for two days in the hospital. I know about the time you stole jeans from the Macy's store with Dan and sold them, and how you got caught." Our eyes met in the mirror. "I know that you lost your friend." He spoke more to himself now in the mirror. "And I know exactly how you lost him."

"You don't know shit!"

"I know your whole life, Brogan."

"Well, that's just spectacular. I don't know a thing about either of you."

"As well you won't, Siddhartha."

"What are you talking about?"

"Sometimes, Brogan, giving voice to the past resurrects it. Besides, the past is the past, and it no longer exists. Let it be silent and then we can get on with our lives. Sometimes, ignorance of the situation is the safest and happiest route. Keep your guard up."

"I did."

"Frank has always been a very long and dysfunctional story to me, a sort of Anna Karenina or Don Quixote. The thing about it, I'm going to miss the ending of that story. And that is something I've always been very curious about."

"Are you going somewhere?"

"It's likely," he said. "It's like this, when the universe was born, the potential was enormous. Entropy was high. It expanded, formed worlds, revolved around suns. Stars cooled and died. Entropy is slow and deceitful, it goes on undetected, but eventually the heat will dissipate. Eventually everything will cool and die. Get it?"

"I don't," I said. "What does that even mean? I'm not interested in any more mysteries. I'm cleaning up my own blood, in case you hadn't noticed."

"Frank came back to the states when they rehabilitated me. He said he came back to help me, and he certainly did. But I know people too. I know people who knew him down there. He needed to get the hell out of town. Another year down there and he was either going to be dead or in jail for the rest of his life."

"Down where?"

"Puerto Rico. Frank always sent me money, but I was drinking back the butter faster than he could send it. I wish he had come back sooner. He might have saved my ass."

"Looks like he did."

"Not quite," Bogota said.

"I am a grave man," he said in his most Shakespearean voice.

I took a step back. He was adjusting his hair again, this time trying to cover a lesion on his forehead.

"Don't worry, knucklehead. I gotta bleed on you or fuck you in the ass. Neither of those is going to happen."

That disease was new at the time. It was a death sentence. No one understood it. On the news, they called it the "gay plague." At school, the teachers used it as a threat to steer us away from sex.

"Are you dying?"

"Aren't we all, Brogan?"

"What about the boxing? I could have hit you."

"Not a chance," he said, laughing quietly.

"How did it happen?"

"How do any of these things happen? It could have been a needle. It could have been one of the transfusions. Or it could have been, you know what. Who the hell knows?"

"I'm so sorry."

"Shut up. Don't get soft on me. Someone has to be around for him. When I was coming off of everything, they put me away. I had the shakes real bad in the ward. He would come to visit, reading me the goddamn Reader's Digest Word Power, and then plays like King Lear, Richard III, and Macbeth. I hated it. I never knew what the hell anyone was saying in those plays. I never thought I would have such a good vocabulary. I can still remember stupid shit, like 'nefarious.' Do you know what that means?"

"Evil."

"It means evil. That's right, you smartass little shit."

He packed up his makeup supplies.

"I'm good with it. I lived a thousand lifetimes. It's just that, on certain days, I feel like I'm going to miss things. Weird shit. Like peaches. Like canned peaches with whipped cream. You know, the real sweet kind." He smiled. "Like conversation over freshly baked bread when the sun is rising."

"Sounds poetic to me," I said.

"Not gonna happen. I never liked bourbon," he said, laughing. "Not for me. You, on the other hand, there's hope."

"Does he know?" I ask.

"Of course, he knows. It doesn't take a genius. Like many things with Frank, he lives in denial. Frank's just blowin' in the wind. He is good at it. You of all people will learn that."

Bogota fixed his hair in the mirror. "Maybe you're right about it being a dirty trick. And I apologize, which is something that I rarely do. But I'll tell you, you did damn good. Keep your hands up though after you throw the right. Always protect yourself."

He left me to the cold tile and stainless steel.

I DROPPED SOME COINS into the slot, and after a few rings, I heard the low, sweet voice.

It was the same sweet voice, a sort of whisper that Linda had on the nights when she and I were alone. She would tell me everything late at night, sitting on the back porch and watching the moon. She couldn't sleep most nights in the house, waiting for whatever show my father would act out, and wondering whether he would return at all. She could never sleep without him there. On those late nights, we stayed up and watched the night sky unfurl into morning, her bundled shape against the railing of the porch, ducking her head between her knees to subdue a cry. In her eyes, leaving my father was the sanest, and yet nonsensical thing to do. At night, I would hear her quiet phone conversations, trying to reason it out. Her heart was breaking. I would guess at who was on the other end of the phone conversation. She defended Will. She always defended him. "It will only be for a short time. My god, no. Divorce!" she would say. "We don't do divorce." It would be tough for her to afford the apartment, and she knew it. It would be tough for her not to see me every day. She would worry. "I've gone as far as I can go," she would say.

And now hearing that same strained voice on the telephone, that desperate and scared whisper, I could tell she was there again. She had gone as far as she could go.

"Hello," Linda's voice said. "Hello?" she said again. "Brogan, is that you? Put Frank on the phone."

I could hear the low baritone of my father's voice over the background prattle of dishes and voices and clinking glasses.

"Is anyone there? Are you okay? Where the hell are you?" Linda asked. "I don't care anymore. I just want you back here."

The phone was wrestled out of her hand.

"I'm informing the police of an abduction. Do you understand what that means?"

"Will."

"Don't call me that!"

"You said it was my decision. I'm eighteen tomorrow."

"You are blowing it, Brogan. We work our whole lives to set you up and you're blowing it. But that is a disappointment that I'm used to," he said.

"I know what I'm doing," I said.

"I spoke to Brother Michael," he said. "What were you thinking, Brogan? What are you trying to prove?"

"Did everyone come for Thanksgiving?"

"You are being suspended."

On the road, we had passed a thousand Seton Preps. I could hear the doubt in Will's voice. His voice never carried doubt. The work at Seton Prep was easy for me. It was a walk in the park. The world was still open, and I had no need for graduation gowns, and speeches by Valedictorians, and nods to M.I.T.. The institution of Frank, the academy of his will and deliberation were lessons enough, and not delivered with Novocain. Brother Big had called home. Seton Prep was going to suspend me. Fuck them. I wore it as a trophy. Perhaps M.I.T. would have something to say about that. It didn't matter much anymore anyway. Not after the strip clubs, and the gambling halls, and the fistfights. Somewhere in the deep reaches of my soul I found a life that I wanted. I wasn't quite sure what that life was. We had physically travelled only a short distance, but I had aged in experience. I had knowledge now. Will would be terribly disappointed. Linda would be a lunatic. Dan would have approved. He would have given that familiar nod, the one where his mouth turned up in a smirk and his eyes stared back at you over his sunglasses.

"Will. I'm not coming back. Not now."

"You take that money, and you get on the next bus, taxi, airplane, fucking rickshaw, and get back here. Or I'm coming."

I held the phone to my face. The receiver was cool, and it felt good against the welts that were forming from the fight.

Beyond the rest stop, I could see Frank looking for me. He and Bogota had gone to use the bathroom, and they were now standing in the parking lot and looking around.

"Brogan, put Frank on the phone."

I didn't answer. The operator was asking for my change.

"Put him on the goddamn phone!"

"WHAT IS IT** that the Buddha says?" Frank says, turning to Bogota. "Don't be attached to the results, and you won't get fucked." Frank said.

"Yup, something like that," Bogota said.

Frank had five large on the Detroit Lions to win. The vig was ten percent on this bet, five hundred dollars. It's the juice. It is the kick in the ass after you've already lost. It is the price of doing business for him. If Frank wins, it's even money. He can double the five. If the Lions win, Frank will go a full rack on the Cowboys' game. That's ten grand. Frank wrote notes in his notebook while he was driving. The Chevy swerved in and out of the lanes. Frank had to be shitfaced. I could smell the liquor on his breath from the back seat.

We refilled the Chevy with gas. Frank announced, "We have exactly five minutes to piss, and then the egg has hatched." Bogota and I pissed. Five minutes passed. Frank was still on the phone. It was nearly kickoff for the Cleveland Browns game. Frank got the bet in and skipped to the car like a grade school kid. The egg had hatched.

"Cleveland is doomed," Frank said.

"So are you," Bogota said.

"Not this time. No way. I got the jackal in my pocket this time. No way that you're shittin' on my luck. By the way, what time do you have?" Frank asked.

Bogota looked down at the gold Rolex watch on his wrist and smiled back at Frank.

"That's right," Frank said.

We exited in South Carolina and wound through the country roads.

"Where are we going?" Bogota finally asked.

"Ah. The overwhelming question."

Bogota sighed and rubbed his temples.

"'I should have been a pair of ragged claws scuttling across the floors of silent seas,'" Frank quoted.

"Goddamn right you should have," Bogota said.

I wasn't used to these open expanses of country, and when we finally arrived at the house, it was like a surprise. The house was set back from the road, a cyst on the side of a hill. The shutters were in ruin. The yard was littered with old and rusted furniture. Shoots of grass invaded the walk. The picket fence was in disrepair. The afternoon was getting on. Frank needed to get to a television. It seemed a long way to travel when we could have just stopped at another bar.

"I need you to wait here for a bit," he said to me.

Frank left the car and was on the porch in seconds tapping at the door.

"Where the hell are we, anyway?" Bogota asked.

Frank knocked and a woman answered the door. They had an argument. She looked past Frank and looked at me and stopped dead on the porch. Even at a distance, I could see her green eyes.

"Holy shit," Bogota said when he recognized her. "This is going to be interesting."

A younger woman appeared from the house also. She looked a bit older than me. She had her hair pulled back and she wore a United States Marines sweatshirt. The older woman finally just shrugged, then she threw her arms in the air, shouted, and stepped inside.

Bogota took out his makeup kit, lowered the visor, and studied himself in the mirror.

"What in God's name are we doing here?" he asked more to himself.

"Is your real name Jerome?" I asked.

"Yes," he said. The colored pencils and brushes clicked together as Bogota fingered through the kit. Bogota was now only a shadow in the dying afternoon. I felt terrible pity for him. I couldn't tell him that. He would want to crack me one. That would be letting my guard down. That would be dropping my hand on the overhand right. It was hard to imagine Bogota disappearing. He would never fit inside the normal dimensions of a coffin.

He pruned himself, applied a thin layer of foundation to his face. He painted over the base coat with blues and pinks and sharpened his eyes with black pencils. He was his own masterpiece.

"I don't let anyone call me that. So do both of us a favor and don't use it."

I was shocked that he answered the question.

Frank was on the porch once again and waved us inside.

"I suppose we ought to see what this lunatic wants to do now."

"Come on! We're almost at half time! Hurry up for the sake of all that's holy," Frank said, hustling us along.

"Hold up a minute," Bogota said to Frank. "Is this a good idea?"

"What? It's Thanksgiving. We're starving. The game is on. Let's go."

"No, really, Frank."

"It's a good idea. C'mon. We're going to miss the beginning of the second half, and I'm fucking starving, and this kid needs some food. He's so skinny that he looks like he only has one side. Jesus, you could dodge rain drops. Is Will feeding you?"

"Yes."

The home was like an upside-down ship, with huge, exposed beams that ran the expanse of the bow. The rooms were cluttered with furniture that were being stripped and recoated with primer and paints. A heavy scent of turpentine floated in the workspace. An old wardrobe was missing a door. The rusted hinges were spread on a dirty blanket. I stopped to look around the room. I recognized one of the photographs on the coffee table. It was Will's favorite photograph of me. We were outside a lake house in early September. Will was pretending to bear hug me from behind, and we were both laughing.

Distant voices spoke from the kitchen. The faint smell of turkey and potatoes made my stomach yearn. In the kitchen, Frank was seated at a metal table. He had positioned an old black and white television with huge rabbit-ears antennas on a chair with the volume turned up slightly. He kept moving the metal and tried to get good reception.

"This is a nightmare," Frank said, turning dials while the picture emerged from a haze of crosshatched lines.

The woman with the green eyes wasn't expecting company. She was upstairs. The turkey wasn't much bigger than a chicken.

The younger woman sat at the table with her hands folded on her lap. She wore a patterned dress now, and her hair was now in two pigtails. Her eyes were like a raven's, her pupils huge and black, darting from me to Frank to Bogota. Her mouth was slightly open in an expression of disbelief.

The green-eyed woman returned and danced across the floor and hugged Bogota for a long time. "Look at you," she said to him. "Much better than the last thing that they did to your nose. You look perfect." She cupped his chin. "You've done it. You are beautiful." She drew her hand across his face, down the sloped, chiseled cheekbones. "The statue of David, sculpted out of an imperfect piece of marble." He didn't like to be touched, but he allowed her to run her hands across his lips and forehead. She gently shielded his eyes. He raised a hand to stop her, but she grabbed his arm and gently brought it to his side. "Think of a dream. A place where you can go," she said. His hands were by his side. He was defenseless. He did what she said. It looked like he was thinking of a dream. He opened his eyes and smiled. Bogota didn't smile much.

"Look at your lips, and your hair!" she said to Bogota.

"Diane, are you good with all of this?" Bogota whispered to her.

"All right, enough with the groping of one another. Introductions. Brogan, this is Diane," Frank said, pointing to the green-eyed lady. "And this is Eva, your … um … cousin, I guess."

"Nice to meet you both." I said, and then I turned to Diane. "So does that make *you* my aunt?"

Diane hesitated for a long time while still looking at Bogota. She took a deep breath. She wore no shoes. The bottoms of her feet were black from the dirty floor. She released Bogota and turned to me. "Brogan," Diane said. "Brogan," she said again. She took both of my hands and stared me up and down. "I never thought," she said. We looked into one another's eyes with an odd, powerful, and timeless current. Her legs wobbled a bit, and I figured her to be a bit tipsy by the display of mostly empty wine bottles.

Diane had an overabundance of flesh that cloaked the subtle beauty beneath. It was a badge of severe abuse: food or drugs or alcohol. Her hair was frosted, tangled and unkempt; her nails were painted, but chewed.

She moved her hands across my shoulders and then my neck. She held my head the way that Linda would when she was proud of me or about to tell me something very important. She tried that same move on me that she used on Bogota. She put her hand across my eyes. She shielded my eyes with her palm, stumbling a bit from the wine. "Think of a dream," she said. "A place where you can go." She suddenly drew me in close and began to cry, quietly at first, and then building into heaving sobs. I began to sweat terribly. I put my arms back around her and looked to Frank and Bogota and Eva. She broke free from me and left the room to clean herself up. Everyone was silent and studying the floor.

"What the hell was that all about, Frank?" I asked.

"Women are stochastic," Frank said.

"What does that even mean?"

"Estrogen variables," Bogota said.

"Do either of you ever not speak in riddles?" I asked. But they were onto something more important. The football game was at half time.

"Are you on school vacation?" Eva asked.

"I guess," I said. "Are you?"

"I suppose. I'm not sure if I feel like going back," she said.

"Oh, yes you are," Diane said, returning to the room.

She sipped at her glass of red wine and stirred the green beans. She seemed composed. In fact, she now seemed lightened by the company. Her stolen and weighted glances touched on my shoulders where her hands were just moments ago. I could still smell the dish soap on her hand from when she covered my eyes. Bogota sat down at the table. Diane poured more wine, and Frank made jokes.

"What's red and dingle dangles?" he asked Diane.

She played along. "Gee, I don't know."

"A red dingle dangle!" Frank said matter of fact.

Diane turned on the radio. Bogota leaned back in a chair, almost snapping the spine with his enormous weight.

"So," Frank continued, "What is blue and dingle dangles?"

Diane cupped her chin and gave her most pensive look. This was an old game between them. "A blue dingle dangle?"

"No," Frank said. "They only come in red," he and Diane said at the same time with a deep and warm smile.

This was a different Frank. He was not pacing and wringing his hands and chewing on his mustache. He was slack and emanating a glow, and when he looked at Diane there was an electricity. The kind that I felt and saw between Will and Linda. She ducked her head and then stared up at him beneath her falling hair. It was the kind of look that could kill a mortal man.

Sam Cooke crackled onto the radio, belting out "You Send Me." Diane lowered the television and turned up the radio. Frank began a slow dance by himself that was both amazingly rhythmic and hilarious. Frank asked for Diane's hand, and she shook her head "No." He waltzed off by himself, still coaxing his imaginary partner. He sang the song, and his voice was perfectly in tune. When he returned a second time, she accepted without hesitation. They knew one another's steps. They were graceful and effortless, gliding across the kitchen. Eva asked for Bogota's hand, and they danced also.

He took only a few steps and then handed Eva over to me. Eva was tense and erect in my awkward arms. "How did you get those bruises?" she asked.

"I got into a stupid fight," I said looking over at Bogota, who stared unapologetically right back at me.

"I got into a fight once," she said.

"It wasn't what I thought it would be," I said.

"I've found that to be the case with many things," she said.

"Like what?"

"I don't know. Family. Religion. Sex."

"Sex?"

"Yeah. You know. Fucking."

I wasn't sure how to respond to that. I looked over to see if anyone is listening, but Frank was looking over Diane's shoulder, absorbed by the TV, and Bogota was looking at his reflection in the stainless-steel toaster. Diane had her eyes closed and was close to Frank's chest.

"It's more like wrestling match. Anyway. We've heard a lot about you," Eva said.

"Really? From who?"

"Frank always talked about you to us."

"Always talked to you about what?"

"He's so proud of you," she said.

"I've just met him," I said.

The song was coming to a close, and Eva slipped away from me and sat back down, staring at me with her mouth slightly open.

Diane fixed a makeshift meal – there were only three dishes when Linda would have made twenty - turkey, mashed potatoes, green beans. She poured even more wine and asked me if I wanted any. Wine is for women.

"I'll have a beer."

"He's a beer guy," Frank said. I was certain that I was the latest, but would not be the last on a very long list of advocates of Frank's theory of alcohol.

Frank broke from the makeshift meal and hovered by the luminescent glow of the television, working his hands close to the bone. He sat and watched the game closely. The Browns were making a contest of it. Matt Bahr was going for a forty-four-yard field goal. The program switched to a commercial break. Frank chewed on his hand.

"Goddammit, Frank," Diane said in the most painfully loving voice that made it seem the world was breaking into pieces. She was fixed on the loaded plates. "Goddamnit to hell."

"You can't stop a horse—" Frank started.

"I know, Frank. You can't stop a horse halfway through the water, but you sure as shit can shoot one and put it out of its misery," Bogota said.

"That's a bit drastic," Frank joked, but Diane was not getting the humor. "I've got a good ride going on this one. Let it play out."

"We are having dinner," Diane said. "It can wait."

The broadcasters were back from commercial break, and Bahr was lining up for three points. Frank was hypnotized.

"By the way, I'm not giving him a beer. He's just a kid," she said.

"Not after this weekend," Frank said.

"Yes," Diane said. "I know."

We were all joined in Frank's madness and watching to see what the outcome would be. Bahr went wide right and missed the game tying field goal. Frank leaped from the chair and thrust a fist in the air.

"That is what I mean about football!" He stood and seemed more to be talking to himself. "Theater of Dionysus. This is the great Globe itself. All improvised. The perfection of humans' performance."

"All the world's a stage," Bogota said. He held the toaster still. I wondered if he was envisioning a smashing that toaster on Frank's forehead.

Diane served us dinner. She gave me a beer. She dug out an old bottle of Maker's Mark bourbon from the cabinet and poured Frank a shot. Bogota had coffee. Frank didn't eat. He smoked his cigarettes and wrote down equations in his notebook. It looked as though he was just doing simple math, adding his numbers, making predictions, doing whatever it was he did.

"Goddamn that was a close game," Frank said. "What do you think, kid?" he said turning to me. "Dallas is a real shit show this year. If you were a betting man, what would you do?"

"I don't bet," I said.

"Yes, you do," Frank said. "The apple orchard."

"That's not the same."

"Make a decision."

"It's really not that important."

"Why are you asking him, Frank?" Diane said.

I wanted to challenge him. I wasn't getting this whole thing. We were miles from home. I wanted an adventure. I wanted to prove something. Frank traveled a long way to find me, and now the only real conversation that we were having was about a stupid football game. Dan would have had a lot to say. Dan would have dug up graves and ridden through L.A. With the top down.

"It's everything," Frank said.

Diane cleaned up the dishes. By now, back in New Jersey, I'm sure that Uncle George would be gearing up with a few shots of Jack Daniels and settling into the second match of the day, the Dallas Cowboys versus the Philadelphia Eagles.

"I need a phone," Frank said to Diane.

Linda was bowed and defeated, the heaviness of Frank was like a hundred-pound weight around her neck, dragging her into the dirt.

"It's not what you think," Frank said.

"What is it then?"

"We can leave," Bogota said. He stood up and motioned me with a head nod.

"Leave where? Let him stay," she said to me. "And you stay!" she said to Bogota.

"Can't you just enjoy our time together?" Eva asked. "Can you just stop," she said to Diane.

"It's all set," Frank said. "Everything is set."

"You have to stop sometime. A phone? You want a phone?"

"Forget it. I'll cancel the whole thing. We'll have a great weekend. We can stay here," Frank said. "C'mon sweetheart. It will be alright."

"It's just the same shit pot with you, Frank. The same old boring and dangerous shit pot. Phone's in the other room. Do what you got to do," Diane said. She left the dead carcass of the turkey on the table and left.

"I'm in for Dallas. It's their day. If I can get Sal to give me eight and a half, then I'm in for a full rack. What do you think?"

No one answered.

"Come on, Goddamnit. Say something. Anyone?"

Bogota looked down at the table. "You're ten grand up. And now you want to ride that. This is crazy."

"Dallas with eight and a half. They can't lose every game this year. Dallas owns Thanksgiving. Bogota? The new kid is QB today. Anyone? Say something. Fuck!" He looked around the room.

Frank stood, and wringed his hands together. He picked up his notebook and referenced his notes. "No Goddamnit. It's not Dallas."

THE LIVING ROOM was a makeshift workshop where Diane stripped down her old furniture and restored it. The lights were low. She sat on a stool. Her wine was on the floor. She was surrounded by old rags and tools.

An old sideboard had been sanded down. She rubbed the side with a rag and sang to herself. We heard Frank making his case on the phone in the other room.

"I'm sorry. I just need to get away from all that mania," she said. "Look at you. You're almost a man now." She stopped sanding the table and just looked at me the way that she had earlier.

"What is this all about?" I asked. "Why am I here?"

"I can't answer that for you. I am just as surprised as you are," she said.

From the kitchen, the volume had been turned up. Frank let out a big "Whooh!"

"It's your birthday on Sunday," she said.

"Well, that's what I mean. How would you even know something like that?"

"I was there," she said and laughed. She was very drunk. "We all were."

She was talking nonsense. I kind of wanted to get the hell away from all of these lunatics, but we were in the middle of the country.

"What do you do with all of this stuff?" I asked, looking around the room.

"I sell it," she said. "I find these old broken-down pieces. I strip them down and get rid of the old layers. Then I restore them to their natural state. Like that one," she said, pointing over to the same sideboard. "I fix the doors, the drawers, the hinges." She ran a hand across the front of it and picked at a notch in the wood. "This piece is a hundred years old. 1889. What has this piece seen? Imagine what was going on in the world when someone decided to make this. It's astounding."

She rubbed the top of the sideboard with a cloth soaked in turpentine.

"I think that is why I do this. To feel the stories that were there once. To give it a rebirth. To hand it over to someone else. Someone who will take care of it. Someone cared enough to put everything they had into making this at one time, and I want it to live again."

FRANK HAD HIS bet in. I could hear him in the other room. He didn't get his eight and a half points. The Vegas line was six. Frank got seven. He felt confident. He put a full rack on the Eagles giving seven. He said the Cowboys are made for Thanksgiving Day. He said the Cowboys have a hotshot new quarterback, but he hasn't found his groove yet. "Fuck you," he said into the receiver, "I should just go even on the line."

The screen door slammed. Bogota was out on the porch watching the moon. I could see him pacing. The sound of Frank's voice on the phone was like jabs and uppercuts to him. Near the window, a staircase led to an open loft. Eva was seated on the top step. She had changed into a pair of jeans and a loose-fitting red sweatshirt.

"You can join us," Diane said to Eva.

"No, thank you," Eva said.

She stood up on the stairs. "Do you want to see my room?" She said to me.

"Sure."

I left Diane and joined her. Eva sat down on her bed and smoked a cigarette.

"I heard you are going to a big-time school next year," she said. Her bedroom wall had posters of the Marine Corps. I expected pop bands. Her window was propped open to release the smoke, and the cool air felt good. I took a seat on the floor.

"It's a good school," I said.

"I'm going into the service when I'm old enough," she said.

It didn't fit her. She was a prim and petite girl who would have no business in the armed forces. Nothing made sense here.

"You're not applying to colleges?"

"'Waste of time,' Frank says. Plus, I think that I would be a good soldier. That's why I'm not sure that I want to return to school. I'll just wait out my birthday and then enlist. I would be the perfect honeybee. I just need to believe in the hive."

I was waiting for the Queen of Hearts to emerge from the closet and shout, "Off with his head!" I was waiting for the rabbit to check his pocket watch. Maybe I would join Frank's mad tea party downstairs.

"You sound just like the rest of them," I said.

Downstairs, Frank shouted something unintelligible at the football game, followed by a string of curse words. Eva had an ear cocked toward the stairs. She shook her head. "He's not always like this."

The night air now made the house cold, and the damp clung to the blankets and walls. All of her femininity had been removed from the room. No scent of perfume. No pinks or curtains. But still she was dainty in that red sweatshirt, compact, like a geranium with her flowering cheeks and pomp of reddish blond hair.

"There really is a lot that I like about him. We've been through a lot with him. Do you have a girlfriend?"

"Why does everyone always ask me that?"

"I just want to know about your life."

"Do you have a boyfriend?"

"I did," she said. "He's in the Marines now."

She had an old phonograph player and a stack of records. I fingered through them. Her taste was lacking. Dan would have puked. It was mostly the popular MTV music of the day. I found a familiar record, London Calling, The Clash. Perfect. I pulled the album out and played it.

She stood and started to wave her head from side to side and bounced with the music. She was free and alive in the music, and the veneer of shyness and uncertainty slipped from her. She twirled and drew me into the dance. When the song was over, she turned down the music. She went to a closet and pulled out an old shoebox filled with photographs. She patted the bed, indicating that she wanted me to sit down next to her. "Look at this one." She held up a photo of two young men near a bridge. They were wearing what looked like matching black leather jackets.

"That's him!" I said. I could see the ghost of that lost kid, his hair short and cropped, an angular and large Roman nose, the burgeoning shoulders. It was definitely Bogota, or he may have been Jerome then. "God, what happened to him?"

"I can remember him before all of the surgeries," she said. "He used to wear a wig. Then he just grew his hair out, and, well, you can see the rest."

"But why?"

"I'm not sure, really. I think something happened to him when he was younger. That's the rumor."

Frank was the other boy in the picture, without his mustache and with hair, a blondish mop above his bluish eyes.

"Something happened?"

"I guess it's something he doesn't like to talk about. He doesn't like to answer questions."

"No shit."

She rummaged through the box, examining pictures until she found what she was looking for. "This is your grandfather and grandmother," she said, holding another photograph, an old black and white picture that was frayed at the edges. The man, my grandfather, was very tall and thin, and I could see Will in his features.

It was their wedding day. He stood erect in the hall of the VFW. The woman, Sophia, was my grandmother. She had her hair up, and she looked like she was midway through a laugh. She had high cheekbones that pushed forward and accented her big round eyes. Her hair was done up in a beehive.

"I met him once," Eva said. "Mom packed us up in the car, and we went one afternoon to meet him. I was much younger, but I knew even then he was not such a nice guy. Mom said it would help us understand Frank. It didn't."

"My grandfather!"

"Yes. He's not very nice."

"I thought that he was dead?"

She just shrugged her shoulders as if it wasn't a big deal, as if she didn't just resurrect a forgotten and unknown immediate member of my family.

"Oh, look at this one!" She handed me another picture of a young couple on the beach and a little girl building a sandcastle. Frank looked to be in his mid-twenties, young and lean. His hair was neatly cropped high on his forehead and was beginning to thin. He was tan and fit, with a diamond smile. Diane was thin in a bikini, her hairstyle was outdated, not teased and blown out, but natural and long and gorgeous. The little girl looked at the camera, distracted from her masterpiece. "I remember the guy that took this photo of us. A short little man that Frank bullied into taking the picture for a dollar. That was Puerto Rico. We lived there for a while when I was a kid. I had a Spanish tutor. In the morning, Frank took me running on the beach. He didn't drink as much then. Then, Frank was in jail for a bit. We would just wait."

"Jail? For what?"

"I think he killed someone. No one could prove it. It was self-defense."

"I'm not sure that I believe that," I said. "He's a lot of things that aren't right, but not a murderer."

"Whether he did or not, we had to get out of town. Mexico was the first choice. We stayed in Cancun at first, and then Playa del Carmen for a while. Que quiere beber?"

"What does that mean?"

"What do you want to drink? Que quiere comer?" She asked. "What do you want to eat?"

"I'm not hungry or thirsty."

"Don't be silly. I'm just showing off my Spanish."

"Perro Negro," I said.

"Black dog," she said and laughed. "What does that mean?"

She walked over to the bureau, opened the drawer, and unraveled a bag of marijuana. She sat nearer the window and packed a one-hitter.

"I know what you are doing up there!" Diane yelled from below.

"Some of us are made for this world," she whispered and lit up the smoke in a one-hitter again. "Some of us aren't. Who are we to judge them? We just love them. Plain and simple. It doesn't make it right. It just is."

"'Why, sometimes I've believed as many as six impossible things before breakfast,' said the Queen of hearts," I said.

Eva was nodding out. She was going to join the Marines, or the Army, or the Air Force.

DIANE WAS ASLEEP on the couch. The ghostly light of the television came from the kitchen.

"Brogan," Frank said. "Come in here."

It was the third quarter. The Philadelphia Eagles were murdering the Dallas Cowboys. The score was seventeen to zero. Frank was leaned back in his chair and gnawing on his hand. The bottle of bourbon was dangerously low.

"You ever watch the games with Will?" He poured the last of the bourbon.

"Once in a while. He loves the New York Giants. He calls Phil Simms a lip-lock lesbian."

Frank laughed at this. "I remember that phrase. He used to go to a lot of the games with The Funkie. Once in a while, they would take me. It was mostly fun depending on which personality came out, depending on whether he got drunk or not. When he went off to the bathroom, Will and I would sneak sips of his beer. We had somewhat of a life with him before your grandmother died."

"Will never said much about either one of them."

"That doesn't surprise me."

"Is he alive?"

"That's a matter of opinion. But hopefully not."

He watched the television intently, even though the football game was now on commercial break.

I think about Will being at home and half out of his skull with my disappearance. We did watch a lot of games together. Mostly, I watched the games for his sake. I somehow didn't see them as great theater. I missed the boat on the human perfection. It was mostly just a lot of stop and start action, long drawn-out moments of decision making. Often, I would read a book while Will screamed at Phil Simms on the television. Will assigned his virtue to that team, his supreme and utter devotion to that Sunday ritual, not to be interrupted, and not to be discolored in any way. He would look at me and shake his head. "Don't you get it?" he would ask. "Did you see that pass!" I would look up and say all I could say. "What's the score, Will?"

Did he know that his own father was alive?

Frank leaned forward in the chair, his hands clasped, an eyebrow arched. "You have to understand the chaos of football."

The Eagles scored another touchdown, and Frank winced. "That's got to hurt. Everything points to a Dallas victory, and yet here we are seeing the worst ass-kicking in the history of Thanksgiving football."

"So why do you bet on it?"

"When you say 'bet,' it doesn't do it any justice. This is not just a dog pissing on any tree, this is the butterfly flapping its wings," Frank said.

"Why did you drag me halfway down the coast to watch a football game?"

"It was the right time."

"What am I doing here? Why is there a picture of me here? How do they know Will and Linda so well? I know that Bogota says not to ask questions, not to resurrect the past, but this is all very confusing. Is this your family, Frank? Is that your daughter? Did you kill someone? This is one big roller coaster ride."

Frank didn't answer right away. He hadn't thought this whole thing through. He didn't think I would have questions. His hand was bleeding, from chewing on the side of it.

"It's not that simple of an answer, Brogan," he said.

"Only if you complicate it," I said. "I'm not looking for the right answer. I just want the real answer. This whole thing is off somehow."

"You're a smart kid. A bit of a smartass, but a smart kid. Probably got a perfect SAT score," he said.

"I did," I said. "They accused me of cheating, so I took it again."

"Then you know the meaning of illegitimate," Frank said.

Bogota came back in from outside. He had been walking for an hour. He looked at the screen and shook his head. "That's just fucking fantastic," he said. "Ten tall on the Eagles, and Dallas is not even on the board."

"I'm winning."

"I know," he said. "That's the worst of it."

The game came to a close, and the Dallas Cowboys had suffered their worst defeat in a Thanksgiving Day game. A great and epic battle. "'Upon Saint Crispin's Day!" "Once more unto the breech, dear friends, once again." Frank said. He had finished the last of the bourbon and was working on the few beers in the fridge. "We should celebrate."

L **ET'S HEAD BACK,"** Bogota said. "Dog tracks don't seem like the best idea."

"Let's put the cabbage on that right now," Frank said and turned to me. "I got a lead on a good run in Naples."

"Do you know how fucking far that is?" Bogota said.

"Then we need to get moving. Kid's here for an education. He's gonna get one. You could learn all that you need to know at a race-track: math, science, and social studies all in one. Even meteorology and geometry. Much better than that science school that you are going to. And a hell of lot cheaper."

"I have a scholarship," I said.

Bogota looked exhausted. After the game, we had gotten what little sleep we could. As usual, Frank didn't look as though he had slept at all.

"I don't want you to go," Diane said.

"The race is at four P.M. tomorrow, babe. We gotta scoot."

The living room was quiet. Diane was poised now, sitting with a stack of papers in her hand. Bogota and I had gathered up the bedding and made neat piles of linen on the armrest. We were jacketed and ready to join Frank. Eva sat on the couch, sleepy eyed and dreamy. Diane stood up and handed Frank a stack of notes that looked like a series of individual letters.

"What? What is this? Your resignation?" Frank said laughing. She didn't answer. Frank took the letters and began to read. He took a seat and read through each individually. He was unable to conjure that charm, unable to manufacture that effortless and never-ending bag of bullshit answers. When he was finished, he sat for a while with his hand on his chin looking out the window.

"And, what? Should I give a shit? What do you want me to do with this?" he said after reading the notes.

"I just think that it may be more important than any dog race-track in Florida." Diane said. She looked to Bogota for help.

"Leave me out of it," Bogota said. "In my opinion, we need to put *the cabbage* on this whole bag of shit."

"Your father is dying," she said. "Make your peace with it."

"How would you know that?" Frank asked her. "And, by the way, he's not my father."

"He raised you," she said. "He was your mother's husband."

"You go then," Frank said to Diane. "Tell him I said 'hi.'"

Frank dropped the mess of papers on the table.

The letters were ripped from one of those black tablet composition notebooks. The pages were smeared with food and coffee. The handwriting was large like a child's and was sloppy. The way that the letters were pieced together, it appeared as though they had been written in separate stages in black and blue and red and green ink. They were sun stained. I gathered them up. I began to read one of them, but they were quickly ripped from my hand.

"What if we didn't come here? What if we never stopped to see you?" Frank said. "When were you going to tell me about this?"

"I'm not sure that I would have. But the road that you are on now, I'm thinking that you needed to know."

Frank ignored her and just looked out the window.

"What road is that?" Frank whispered more to himself. He began to sing softy with an Irish accent. "We are on the one road/ It maybe a long road/ We are on the road to God knows where."

Before we left, Diane went upstairs to Eva's room and came down with her box of photographs. She was crying by now, having felt some sort of betrayal toward Frank. He said that it wasn't like that, that it is best just to let the dead be dead. He opened the box and looked through the pictures. He saw the one of himself and Bogota as kids and laughed and showed Bogota, who had no interest whatsoever. He saw the one of his mother and The Funkie and studied it for a long time.

"I do appreciate what you are trying to do, and I do sincerely thank you for the trip down nutcase highway, but we gotta go," Frank said.

The first of the morning birds were announcing sunrise. My eyes had that stinging pain of interrupted sleep. We said our goodbyes.

"I'm not going to see you again," Diane said to Bogota. She touched his face again and ran her hands across his shoulders and neck. "I just know it."

"I'll see you soon," he said and walked away.

"And you!" She said to me. "Goodbye for now," she said and handed me a sliver of paper with the house phone number. "Let me know when you land." She folded me into her arms and hugged me for a long time.

Eva wanted to take a picture with her Polaroid camera. Frank made her wait while he fetched a bottle of bourbon and a can of beer from the house.

We held the bottles high, and Bogota looked the other way with his arms folded. She snapped two pictures. From the blackness, they morphed into that frozen moment.

"You keep this," she said. "And I'll keep this one." She reached over and kissed my cheek. "Next time I see you, I'll be a sergeant-major."

Diane drew Frank once more to her before we left. She placed her hand over his eyes. She pressed his forehead to her lips. "Think of our dream," she whispered.

Happy Birthday!

Mistakes are like the pits that you find in cherries, a hard and ugly center to a beautiful fruit, the seed that is the beginning. Don't be so quick to spit it out, but chew on it a while, maybe let it knock a couple of your teeth out. Learn from it, and then bury it. Look forward to them, because they are going to happen. Remember sometimes the girls' cherries have pits also. Watch out for those! Remember this too! When you want to say something nasty, stop and think. Just stop. Then decide.

Happy Birthday, Brogan.
Love, Frank

A**LATE AUTUMN FIRE** had reduced the landscape to a barren, grayish-white wasteland. It could have been the moon. It was a dead world of fire-eaten trees that were still standing like lost and confused ghosts.

"What's the dog's name?" Bogota asked, trying to break the monotony and the mounting pressure.

"What dog?" Frank asked. He was deep into his own thoughts.

"The race. What's the dog's name that's racing?"

173

"Still working on that one," Frank said.

"No shit," Bogota said.

"When is he running?"

"Saturday. In the eighth."

"We're not going to make it driving like this."

"We'll make it."

We pulled up to a battle-worn sign for a trailer park that looked like the entrance to Auschwitz. The double-wide trailers were dismal. The inhabitants tried to make them livable. They installed flowerpots and set up small picket fences, but mostly, the trailer park looked like a field of broken and dying barracks.

We walked past one trailer, and the door was suddenly flung open and a naked old man charged at us with sinewy muscles like piano wire and wide and wild eyes. His penis flapped against his thigh like a mouse. Frank grabbed him immediately and had one hand around his throat, and the other ready to knock him out. But the old man simply fell to his knees and begged us.

"My Anthony?" he asked.

"That's not us," Frank said.

"Do you know him?"

Frank's face was drawn in sympathy, and he lowered his hand. "I'm sorry," Frank said.

The old man began to sob, and we left him to his sorrow.

"This is it," Frank said, pointing ahead at a bend in the dirt road.

"I was here once. He didn't know it. Then I thought it would be useless to beat the ever-loving shit out of an old man."

We followed closely behind. I tried to look inside the windows, but they were mostly curtained and dirty. I could feel the weight of this place, a dull hand that pressed on the chest and choked out the oxygen. The sides of the trailer were filthy. One of the windows was missing a pane and was covered with an old piece of cardboard. A small, splintered porch clung to the front. Somewhere, a dog gave a fierce growl.

"Quiet," came the voice from the rocking chair. "Who the hell is it, anyway?"

"It's me."

"Frank?"

This was the loathsome and dirty home of a nearly blind man. Frank wet his lips with some balm. The furniture was old and ragged and unkempt. Sunlight was stunted by the filthy windows. The Funkie fumbled his way through the double-wide, dragging a heavy oxygen tank and tapping his way around furniture with an old pool cue. He was taller than Frank. His bones were like shards of glass beneath a loose-fitting t-shirt. He seemed deluded into the guarantee of another tomorrow, and he wore an arrogant grin. The eyes, unseeing, were not dead yet, as if siphoning out color from the world around him into black holes. His face was a mass of hollows collecting pools of darkening shadows.

"Ah, and so it is Frank, out of anyone, who has come to visit a dying man," he said. He stood and felt his way along the filth of the countertop for guidance. He opened the cabinet and used his sense of touch to find a bottle of gin. He placed the glasses in front of each of us and filled them. I dared not drink it. Those goddamn juniper berries. The Funkie drew heavily on a cigarette and coughed, breathing a deep gurgling sound like water boiling.

"What are you doing here, Frank?" he asked, and he really did seem curious about this, even a bit surprised.

"I'm not sure myself. You look terrific," Frank said flatly.

I was afraid to move all the way into the trailer, so I stayed near the door. Bogota just seemed disgusted to be here.

"Don't be a smartass. Who is there with you?" The Funkie asked.

"Well, you remember Jerome."

"Of course, I do. I thought he never had his own home. Candyass."

"Hello, Mr. Camden."

"Don't give me that bullshit, Jerome. I see someone else there. Who's the boy?"

175

"My name is Bogota."

"Yes, and I'm The Funkie. I know that stupid name. You all always had names for everyone. My ass," he said. "Your mother named you Jerome. I'm calling you Jerome. Who else is there?"

Frank sipped the gin. "That's Brogan."

The Funkie stopped his cigarette midway to his mouth. He was unsure how to respond. He took so long to answer that I wasn't sure if he had suffered a fatal stroke and put himself out of his misery.

"I've heard about you," he said.

"I imagine," I said. That was a strange thing to say. He was, after all, my grandfather. I was starting to jump on the bandwagon of people who did not like this man. I had questions. *Where the hell have you been for eighteen years?*

"Yes, that's him," Frank said. "Living and breathing flesh."

"Is William here?"

"No."

"Where is William?"

"He is in New Jersey," Frank said.

He reached out a bony hand that looked like broken twigs. Out of respect, I stood to shake his hand, but Frank stopped me.

"He's fine where he is."

"Let him come a little closer. I don't see that well anymore. He looks like a strong young man."

"He has his moments," Frank said. "You're dying?"

"So, they say."

"Well, I'm sorry for you," Frank said.

"Ha!" The Funkie croaked. "No, you're not. But that's okay."

He reached into his pocket and pulled out a dirty set of playing cards.

"Those are your cheater cards," Frank said.

"It doesn't matter. I can't see them anymore."

"You could have played them blindfolded."

He shuffled the cards and dealt Frank a hand. "What do we play for?" The Funkie asked.

"Doesn't look like you have much," Frank said.

The Funkie shuffled and reshuffled the cards like he was playing an instrument. He fanned them up into a tent, folded them down, and plucked at the edges. "Do you remember that fourth of July when we got lost in the woods?" He asked. "You and Will were just kids. Scared shitless."

"Yup," Frank said. "I sure do."

The Funkie dealt out five cards. Frank drained the gin, poured himself another, and then picked up his hand.

"I had to take the dog and find you and your brother. Your mother wouldn't sleep until you were both home."

"Yes. I remember it well." Frank said. He was studying his cards, but he looked as though he was somewhere else.

"They were showing fireworks over the Ramapo Reservation. You were both so goddamn little. When I found you, you were lost and cold, and so happy. We stayed and watched the whole show from that hill, the one where the ski lift was."

"Yup."

"Hell of a view from up there. The whole valley."

"It was a peach."

"You and Will sat in one of the ski chairs."

"I remember."

"You were both such a pain in the ass, but that was a great night."

"Sure was. We watched the fireworks. It was amazing. You led us back through the woods and took us to the diner. Will had a great meal. I didn't get dinner. You said it was my fault that we were out there. Remember?" He looked at his hand of cards. "I'll take two," Frank said.

"Being in this condition, there isn't much to do anymore but think. Just to sit and think and remember. I hope you have that one day."

"Must be a hell of a show you're watching."

He scooped up Frank's discard and flipped him two new cards. "Play your hand."

"I'll raise you," Frank said.

"Ha ha. With what?"

Frank laid out his new hand, and The Funkie did the same.

"I still miss your mother, Frank. It's been so long, but I still miss her."

"We all do," Frank said.

They compared their hands. The Funkie put on a pair of glasses that were strapped around his neck. He looked at the two hands and smiled. "Ah, you got 'em on two pair. Not bad. A pussy hand, if you ask me." He took the glasses off again, and now had a bit of smile cracking at the corner of his mouth. He laughed a bit to himself.

"Do you remember the time..." The Funkie began. He fingered the cards and flipped through the deck like a master. But Frank interrupted him.

"You're dealing off the bottom of the deck," Frank said.

"Do you think that matters anymore?"

"Never be an easy mark," Frank said. "Your words. Not mine."

"I'm sure that nothing of mine was yours," The Funkie said under his breath.

Bogota drifted to the door and watched the sullen gray morning. Frank stood and stretched and wandered through the trailer looking at the framed pictures on the wall.

"We gotta get going soon," he said.

A section of the wall of photographs was dedicated to my father and his boxing career. I recognized one photograph from our home. Will was proud and standing outside of an old brick building in Jersey City, with boxing gloves dangling from around his neck alongside a first-place blue ribbon. I picked him out of another photo from amongst his graduating Marine class on Parris Island.

He was thinner. He always boasted that when he graduated from the Marines, he had a twenty-nine-inch waist and a forty-four-inch chest.

"Guess you lost my graduation pic," Frank said.

The Funkie fell into a manic coughing attack, doubling over, viciously fighting to grab his breath. He waved a dismissive hand at Frank.

"There's not much left of this world," Frank said. "Your world."

"It was a life that was lived," The Funkie said. "Nothing more."

"And for you?" Frank said. "You ready to ante up? Are you ready to go then?"

"I'm not sure we are ever ready for that," The Funkie said.

"All of those stories—all that bullshit you think that you remember, and they are great stories—they are just not accurate."

"How so?"

"You did a lot of bad things," Frank said while still staring at the photographs. "And you didn't have to." The words came from Frank like a drip of water in a deep well, ricocheting in the room. "To tell you the truth, I don't know why I'm here. Apparently, you and Diane have been talking."

"No one else gives a damn. Your brother may be dead for all I know."

"Nope, he's alive. He just doesn't give a shit about you. Here's another good story. Stop me if you know this one. That day that we took your gin, it was wrong. We didn't realize how wrong it was, and I admit that it was wrong. You brought ice from the kitchen. You made us keep our hands there until it hurt so bad that we couldn't feel anything anymore. You let William go, but you kept me there longer."

Frank stretched his right hand and flexed the fingers. "Never worked the same," Frank said, looking at his own hand. "Never quite worked the same again. My baseball days were over after that."

"You stole alcohol. What should I have done? Bought you a candy bar?"

Frank squeezed his hand with his missing fingertips. "Never worked the same. Yes. I get that you should have punished us. We deserved that," He released a long breath as if he were trying to calm himself. "But not like that."

The Funkie was quiet.

"'I died as an animal, and I was a man,'" Frank said. "That's from a poem. Rumi. I don't expect that you would know that."

"We both know the truth, Frank. It was never the same after you were born. It killed me."

"I understand," Frank said. "That wasn't my fault. Whatever the past was for you, it had nothing to do with me. Whatever the past was for my mother, it wasn't my fault. And now she is dead. And you are going to be dead soon too."

"This is ridiculous."

"No. It's not," Frank said. "I look around, and I see everything around us, this desperation, this whole life, this boy, my life. None of it is ridiculous. We had all the potential in the world, like a great big bang, endless possibility, fracturing into endless outcomes. All that possibility in a single moment. This is where it led us. To nothing. This is the end for you. I wanted to come here and tell you that I hope you burn in hell when that moment comes, but I can't. I just hope to be rid of you, and I think that is a worse thing to say."

"I raised you like you were my own," he said.

"No, you didn't," Frank said, laughing again. "You were a monster."

"Why are you really here?" The Funkie asked. "I am dying. I have to die here alone. Isn't that enough?"

Frank stared at the photos on the wall. "You must have lost my baby pictures too. Because the whole clan is here, but not a single goddamn picture of me!"

"You were a disgrace."

"I never asked to be here," Frank said. He turned to look at The Funkie and held him in his gaze for a long time.

He came to the pictures of his mother, Sophia, my grandmother, whom I had never met. His hands were on his hips. He let out a long-exasperated breath. "That morning," Frank said.

"I don't want to talk about that now," The Funkie said.

Bogota stepped away from the door and angled an ear toward Frank.

"I tried to save her."

"What are you talking about?" The Funkie asked.

"Do you know why I couldn't?"

"I don't want to know." The Funkie stared into his gin. His eyes were welling up. Bogota was speechless. "I don't want to talk about that," he said again. He couldn't see anymore, but he couldn't escape the memories.

"Do you know how she did it? Because I do."

"She fell asleep and drowned," The Funkie said.

"That's because she took eleven times her prescription for Valium."

"I hate you," The Funkie said.

"I know you do," Frank answered. "But that is okay. You don't have too many tomorrows. So, I'm going to tell you. She did it so that once she started, she wouldn't be able to change her mind and stop. That's why she did it in a bathtub."

The Funkie sank more into the chair, melting into the arm rests. His raspy breath was like a swarm of bees. "Your father was a good man," The Funkie said. "It's hard to accept someone is a good man, when you are not. He came to me and admitted it. He said that he would take care of it. You barely made it into this world. She wanted you."

"A good man? Are you joking? Vinny the Legs? Not too many would agree with you on that one. Don't you see?" Frank said. "I never asked to be here. Do you understand?"

"You were always a reminder to me of my own failing. I tried to accept it."

"Do you understand? There are always three sides to a story. You remember it one way, and I remember it another. And then along comes the artichoke heart."

"And here you are, a common thief, a convict telling me what is right and what is wrong."

"Yes," Frank said. "But at least I know who I am. I also know that I could have made more of this life."

"Well, don't bitch to me, Frank. We all make choices. You didn't need to do time. You took a fall. And then they left you. You chose this life. Only you."

"We've been playing this hand for forty years."

"Then you need to ante up," The Funkie said.

"Even here, one foot in the grave and the other on an oil slick, you are still a mean bastard," Frank whispered.

"We are who we are."

Frank steeled his nerves. He used one hand to stop the other, deformed hand from shaking. You don't taunt the devil. You don't trade leather with a demon. His voice was barely audible when he spoke. "I couldn't get her out in time. Her eyes were wide open. As if she was shocked by what she had done."

The Funkie buried his face in his hands.

"I hope it hurts you. I dragged her out of the water."

"It was an accident. She fell asleep."

"She let go of her shit, in more ways than one. I didn't have the strength to get her out of the tub. She was naked. Where were you? Do you know why your wife had a child with another man? It was because you were a rotten person. You had a black soul. You took out your miserable existence first on her, and then me, and then all of us."

"I didn't do it," The Funkie said.

Frank picked up the photo of his mother again. "You must have done something to make her marry you."

"We were happy."

"Somehow, I don't believe that. And she's not here to tell me," He put the picture down. "Why couldn't it have been you who died then?"

"Don't worry, it won't be much longer."

"Do you expect me to feel sorry for you? You are right. We all make choices. She made a choice not to see him again. And you made a choice to remind me of it for the rest of our lives."

The Funkie leaned on his pool cue.

"I waited there with her. In that shit stink until they came and took her away. Where were you?"

He didn't answer.

"I guess it doesn't matter anymore. You'll be explaining that story soon enough." Frank stood and collected his jacket. He downed the last of the gin. "Good drinking with you again after all these years, Pops."

"I think that you should go now," The Funkie said. He stood and felt his way into the back bedroom. He returned with an oxygen tank and placed the mask over his face and breathed deeply.

"I have one final thing to show you," Frank said.

"I don't think that we have anything more to say to one another."

"Just this," Frank said, "and you will have your lifelong wish. You will never see me again."

Frank walked past Bogota and I and stepped outside.

He poked his head back in. "You wait here," he said to me. "And you also," he said to Bogota.

"Are you coming?" he asked The Funkie.

The old man ripped the oxygen mask from his face and struggled to stand. He walked toward the door. His gray and dying face turned to me and took a long look. That old, broken body was devoid of soul. He was already spent and dead, but breathing yet with hate, the strongest of wills to keep a soul alive, even for a short time.

"You shouldn't have to see this," The Funkie said to me. He grabbed my hand and put a crumpled twenty-dollar bill in it. "Here, take this. Have a happy birthday from your grandfather." He dragged the heavy cylinder behind him. I wanted to help him.

Outside, their voices carried. Bogota and I left the stink of the trailer and followed Frank.

"I wanted you to see this," Frank said and opened the trunk of the car. The old man limped behind the car. He wore a haughty smirk that quickly disappeared when he looked inside. Even with his limited vision, he knew what lay there. He took a step back, trying to steady himself. His eyes grew wide, and he stumbled to keep his balance.

"Frank…" He backed up, sat down on the picnic bench, and drew heavily on the oxygen tank.

Frank laughed. "That's your work right there. Go ahead. Take a gander."

The Funkie shielded his eyes. "This can't be good."

"I've made it now," Frank said. "I've arrived despite you."

"I don't know what to say. You are in trouble. I know it. I want to help you."

"I always knew you were a coward. But I forgive you."

"I don't need your forgiveness," The Funkie whispered, still in shock.

"It's not you I was worried about," Frank said.

The Funkie had folded.

ON MY FOURTEENTH birthday, Frank sent me a postcard with a picture of a greyhound dog racing track in Florida. It was an older picture. The surrounding land was undeveloped at the time, with the half-constructed buildings in the distance rising out of farm tracks like Egyptian Pyramids.

I often held that postcard, imagining that alien world that Frank occupied. On the front of the postcard, muzzled dogs hammered, suspended, toward the finish line. The grandstands were filled with men and women dressed in their Sunday clothes. That strange scene was etched into my mind: triumphant strangers coupled with the disheartened, a hand raised in triumph, a downtrodden countenance embalmed in failure. How in the hell was that supposed to interest me? What does a kid know of dog tracks? It seemed that a fourteen-year-old would be more in tune with superheroes, a dog, or even a sports hero.

Bogota stared out the window, chewing on his fingernails.

"I never knew about you being there. I didn't know that you saw her dead," he said.

"No one did. I kept that wonderful acorn all to myself," Frank said.

"That's a lot to carry around."

"It's an orphaned baby left at the front door of a fun house."

"What?"

"The pup tent of the carnival."

"Frank," Bogota said. He put a hand on his shoulder, but Frank shrugged it off.

"I am haunted."

Frank had not slept in days, and it was finally beginning to show. I saw traces of the cocaine in his mustache. He was being fueled beyond his capacity. The gasoline smell always trailed behind him. At the rest stop, he made more phone calls, and when he returned, he was agitated and confused. I watched Will approach the edge and come back from it. I couldn't see the same happening for Frank. I hated that he was a slave to the monkey. I felt for him that he had to see what he had seen. I knew now why Will never mentioned his mother.

Frank jolted his head from side to side, checking the rearview mirrors.

"You don't have to keep looking," Bogota said. "You know how this works. If you fuck this up, then you can start checking over your shoulder for the rest of your life."

"I'm hoping that they may have given up on me."

"It never should have gone this far. And if you say anything about horses or water, or Shakespeare, or vegetables, or some other nonsensical bullshit, I'm going to punch you in the face," Bogota said.

Thanksgiving was over and retired in New Jersey by now. The plates had been washed. The extra sleeve for the table was stowed away. I felt a severe pang of guilt. I should have been there. I should have spent that time with my father, the man who had made every sacrifice possible for me. The man who had worked two jobs and a midnight shift just to pay for my tuition. I should have picked the turkey at the grocery store, like he had let me do since I could remember.

I should have cleared the table for a mother who awoke at five in the morning every day so that she could make sure that I went to one of the best schools in America. I could have done a lot of things differently. Linda was probably sick with worry. She would probably make excuses to her students for not having corrected all of their exams on time. The woman who had given birth to me, watched over every illness, cleaned every mess, and ensured with every fiber of her being that I was given a chance for success -- I betrayed her. I betrayed them both. Was there any abduction report? Even if it was an uncle, could it be considered a kidnapping? I wasn't certain of the law. Maybe at eighteen, which was only hours away for me, those rules didn't apply. Maybe at eighteen, they figured it was time for me to make my own decisions. My oddness and separation from the world that I knew around me always made me resentful and protective of my autonomy, and now, I saw, aligned me with Frank. And now it was certainly granted to me.

Even though I didn't understand Frank and Bogota's coded exchange, I did understand that there was danger. The last thing Will and Linda wanted was to place me in danger. Now I was running toward it.

We arrived in Jacksonville late. For the first time, it looked as though Frank might just collapse. He booked a cheap motel. Bogota stood guard, taking a seat near the window, parting the shades to peek outside. I took a long shower and washed away the past three days. When I came out, Frank was splattered across the bed and snoring loudly.

"How much farther are we going?" I asked Bogota.

"I've been asking myself that question my entire life," he said.

"Why do you stay here like this? Why did you agree to come along?"

"This is it for me. I don't have anything else. I don't talk about the future anymore." He stopped and considered his answers. "It's funny to think that the day is out there and defined. Kind of like you know your own birthday. What about you?" Bogota asked. "Why do you stay? You really shouldn't even be here."

"I don't really have an answer for that. I thought that I knew when I came. Now I just don't know, but it seems like something that I have to finish."

We slept. I awoke once during the night. In that quiet moment before dawn, I saw Frank near the window, staring out. He looked in bad shape. When I woke up again, they were already in motion.

"it's show time, Kid," Frank said. "Get cleaned up and get your gear." He motioned me outside. I went to the bathroom and splashed some cold water on my face and looked at the reflection that no longer looked familiar. I gathered up my things and left the room. Bogota was already in the car.

"I'm not sure this is such a good idea," Bogota said.

Frank started the car, and we were off again. "Our dog is running in the tenth race. He needs to win. Not place. Not show, but win. We are going to handle some of the competition and give him a little a boost."

After an hour on the road, Frank turned off the highway into a farm, and we followed the road past a line of orange trees. The farmhouse had a lean. It was tilted to the right, like someone propped up on an elbow. The place looked deserted. The only sign of life came from just beyond the field in the back, which were wooden barracks that were used for racing greyhounds. Frank instructed us to wait in the car. The dogs yelped and barked in the distance. Frank opened the glove compartment and took a stack of bills.

"I can only imagine," Bogota said.

A farm hand had come out when Frank approached the house. He had no shirt and a big, hairy stomach that he rubbed constantly in a circle. He scratched his big ass and walked with Frank toward the barracks. They disappeared into a wooden door. Within minutes, Frank emerged and was back into the car. He showed Bogota a syringe that was filled with a clear liquid.

"This is our guarantee," he said.

"Never a sure thing," Bogota said. "Are we really going to do this? What's the plan?"

"If I were you, I would put the whole ball of wax on this one." Frank looked at me in the back seat. "Are you having a good time?"

"I'm not sure," I said.

"It's not a bad thing that we are doing this. I want you to understand that. Some days are lobsters and steaks. Others not so good. I got to do a little something at the track to make sure there is a win for us."

"You don't have to do anything," I said. "That seems like more than the butterfly just flapping its wings."

He gave me a thumbs-up. And then pointed his thumb down.

"That means yes or no."

"Yes, then," I said.

On the drive out from the farm, Frank jumped out from the Chevy and wandered over to a pile of debris near the side of the barn. He worked off a piece of piping from an old, dissembled horse paddock, and hustled back to the car.

WE FOLLOWED HIGHWAY 75 along the western coast of Florida. The sunlight was bright and blinding. Frank tuned the radio from rock and roll to country to a preacher screaming against lust and fornication and gambling. The wind whipped Bogota's long hair.

"We are truly sinners in the hands of an angry god," Frank said.

It was almost 10 A.M. when we turned off the highway. We followed a narrow road until we reached the parking lot of the dog track. It was empty except for the employees and the Mexican dog trainers, who worked in the kennels. They gathered in groups beneath the banyan trees and drank beer and ate lunch. The building was a sickly yellow, and it seemed as though it was dropped here on the way to somewhere more important. Shotgun shacks squatted next to the track, with laundry hanging in the motionless hot morning. Frank got out and took off his jacket. He wore only a ribbed tank top.

"Christ! I've forgotten how hot it is here," he said. "I wonder what rung of Hell this is?"

"I'd say the eighth," Bogota said.

"That was rhetorical, but while we are addressing it, why the eighth?"

"Liars and thieves."

Bogota changed into a black shirt and a pair of black sunglasses, and strangely, he brought a leather jacket. He looked cool and dangerous. I looked like a moron, still wearing my banana yellow T-shirt. It was the only piece of almost clean clothing that I had.

"This place is a real shithole," Bogota said. "You really got a tipoff for this place?"

"This is the one," Frank said.

"Suspect."

Frank was bubbling with excitement and pacing outside the locked door. The lobby opened for beer and simulcast racing at 10:45, and the parking lot was suddenly full. The gamblers were walking from their broken cars, unkempt, unshaven. They carried programs and calculators, all calibrated with the promise of the first race's results. They looked almost as exhausted as Frank.

The floor was a 1970s lime green, and the stools matched. The ceiling was low slung. The women behind the ticket counters were bruised. An old man questioned an invisible friend. Rows of televisions brought news from the simulcast around the country.

"Three beers," Frank said, sidling up to the bar.

"It's ten in the morning," I protested.

"I don't want one," Bogota said.

"Give me three anyway," Frank said to the girl behind the counter.

Post time for the first race was 12 P.M. Here, the monkey was in his natural habitat and gorging himself, feasting on the desperation, gobbling on the wet brains of the disillusioned. Frank bought a program for the races. The announcer's voice came over the intercom, curt and straightforward like an air traffic controller. He introduced the contestants for the first race, and the trainers trumpeted the greyhounds by one by one for a viewing by the spectators and gamblers. The dogs were beautiful, long and slender as the Chevy, racked for speed, perfectly autonomous machines, razor-backed and sleek. Their names were clever. Frank scrolled through the statistics and made calculations. The dogs snorted and kicked up. They wanted to be dogs. The number eight dog, grey and spotted, stepped lively. He bowed his head and gave us a sidelong James Dean-like glance that slayed Bogota and me but didn't affect Frank.

"The eight," I said.

"Shut up," Frank replied. "Goddamnit, I'm trying to focus."

"Definitely the eight," Bogota seconded.

"Your ass," Frank said. "Both of you."

The trainers paraded the dogs past the players. The eight stopped short, crouched into a question mark position, bent over, and took a huge shit on the track.

"Must have had a big Thanksgiving," I said.

"First of all, the eight is the far position, which gives it a hell of a tough shot. Second, he has only placed twice in the last two weeks. Third, and most important, never bet on a dog that shits on the track. Agreed?"

"Who cares?" Bogota said.

"I guess?" I said.

Frank put his pen down and looked over his choices. "All right, listen up. There's a couple of ways that we can approach this. Go the sure route. Harry's Carey, the number 7, is going off at 3/2. She's a sure thing. BatGoat, the number 3, is even money. And, then there is your number 8, Hey Alf, at 42 to 1. We can put one tall on Harry's to win. That's my instinct."

"Let's just throw shit at a wall and pick splotch numbers," Bogota said.

Frank ignored Bogota. "We box the two numbers, the seven and the three. That's an exacta. If they come in first and second in any order, we win. That will be a sweet payoff. Keep quiet now, I'm thinking."

"Frank, we are wasting time here. We got shit to do," Bogota said.

"First, we box the trifecta. I'll tag on your track-shittin number 8, and if that hits, whoah!"

Frank was sweating terribly. He left and returned shortly with a fistful of tickets and a crash course on dog race betting: exactas, win, place, show, and daily doubles. "If our pony comes in first, that's a win, obviously. Second is the place. Third is the show. Got it? You can go across the board and bet a dog to win, place, and show. If he wins, well, you get paid out for all three. We can do that, but I'm sure that he's gonna win. Why lay out three grand? Instead, we got the bitch at a grand to win."

Bogota sat at one of the metal picnic tables outside. He tipped his head back and soaked in the Florida sun.

"I've thought about Florida my entire life, and here we are, working over betting strategies at a dog track." The frustration was starting to build with him. He stretched his arms and legs. He dropped to the ground and started doing wide grip pushups. I had stopped counting after fifty, but it was well past that, and enough to make him almost collapse with exhaustion. He stood back up. "I'm speechless," Bogota said. "The box trifecta is inefficient, Frank. You're betting out of your ass. Disneyland would have been more in line."

Bogota walked away and I followed him to the fence line. He cracked his knuckles and stretched his neck. The dogs were being yoked toward the starting line. "I'm no different. I'm nothing," he said. "I'm a pawn, not even a bishop or a rook, just a piece that gets moved around and thrown into the fight as fodder. I don't want to be here."

"It's just a track," I said.

"It's a noose," he said. "And don't be fooled you are too."

A bland sounding announcer broadcasted the post. The dogs barked like maniacs. Their sudden compulsion to chase a rabbit down and kill it went far beyond any other of their basic needs: that aberration of the canine mind, solely focused and attuned to the single snap of that door opening and that blinding red rabbit, that elusive whatever, attached to the rail, tempting with earthly delight, and forever unattainable. They reminded me of Frank.

The crowd arched toward the railing. Frank stubbed out his cigarette.

"Party time," he said.

The doors opened and the dogs broke in an explosion of mad, spastic speed, tripping over their own feet, righting themselves, and chasing the lurching metal rabbit with all the ferocity and passion of their pumping bodies, a lustful stampede of violent locomotion. In thirty seconds, they were racing down the final leg. The crowd rose to its feet and screamed. The moans of the losing gamblers sounded like a dying battlefield.

"Holy Christ!" Frank said.

"What now?" Bogota said.

"We hit it," Frank said. "The win and the trifecta."

"You gotta be shittin' me," Bogota said.

"Ha! Funny. You see that I tagged on your stinking, shitting eight to show."

"Bullshit," Bogota said, and went back to sunning his face.

"I'll be goddamned, I think he did it."

It was a photo finish. The eight and the six were locked at the finish, and the powers that be were measuring snouts. A hush came over the crowd. A man in a prim and immaculate suit hugged a much younger girl to his chest. An old man with a Yankees cap shook terribly while trying to adjust his thick eyeglasses.

It was official. Seven, three, and eight.

"The eight went off at 32 to 1," Frank said.

Next to the trifecta light on the big board is the official payout, $1,122.19. Frank also had one tall on the seven to win.

"This kid may be a prodigy!"

Frank went to collect. We eventually did have one of the beers that Frank had recommended earlier. We were caught up in the carnival. Three races went by quickly. We couldn't lose. Frank said that it happened to all the old warhorses at one time or another. You just have that day when you are unstoppable.

"The universe aligns into the singular point of light, and it flows out with such brilliance that it scorches your retinas and makes you see halos for the rest of your life," Frank said.

"We are killing it," I said to Bogota. "Frank is on a roll!"

"Yup," he said.

"You don't seem too excited."

"I'm not."

The deep furrows of his brow formed cracks in his shaped and orderly exterior. The anger was seeping out and invading his posture and the air around him. His normal composure, even in the presence of Frank's ever maddening world, gave way to violent clenching and unclenching of his enormous hands.

"You look angry," I said.

"Chipper."

"I'm confused."

Bogota loosened his hands and shook his arms, trying to dispel the building rage that was seizing up that huge engine.

"I'm not surprised."

"How is Frank winning - prodigiously - in any way bad?"

His head swiveled on his neck, slackening up his shoulders. "Do you feel good now?"

"What? About what?"

"*Prodigiously.*" Bogota said locking his hands together and stretching out his arms. "All better now?"

"All better about what?"

"Listen you smart little shit. What happens when you give a toddler an open bottle of bleach? He drinks. A box of matches? He lights the house on fire." He was bent down and looking directly into my eyes. "How about a loaded shotgun?"

I couldn't look directly at him. He had reached critical mass and was seconds from exploding. It was best to shut up and take my hand off the detonator. We had successfully bucked the odds, and he was mad.

"A prodigious amount of pain and suffering follows," he said. "Inescapably, that is what will happen." I looked up to find he had left my gaze and that he was getting ready to go somewhere. "We have to move now." Bogota was many steps ahead, when he abruptly stopped and turned. "Did I use that word right?"

"What word?"

"Prodigious."

During the fourth race, Frank had a change of heart and quickly sent me to the betting line. It was four minutes to post, and the line was moving slowly. In front of me, an enormously fat man swayed backwards, looking as though he was going to fall over. I stepped to one side and waited, but he righted himself, and the line continued to move forward. Two minutes to post. If I didn't get the bet in, Frank would crucify me. He was on a roll. You don't mess with a man on a roll.

The huge man dabbed at his forehead, lurched forward, snapped himself back, and then came crashing down onto the green tile. His head cracked onto the floor. His eyes rolled into the back of his head. He was gagging on his own tongue, and the sound was squishy. The room was silent. A man from another line snatched the tickets out of his hands and moved toward the door.

Still one minute to post.

"How old are you?" the woman asked me.

"Eighteen."

I stepped over the body of the fat man and laid down $100 on the two to win and $100 on the two and four straight for the exacta.

We won again on the exacta but lost on the win.

"That is just the law of the jungle, Brogan," Frank said when I told him about the falling man. "You did the right thing. Don't feel bad."

"I think he had a seizure," I said.

"'Nature red in tooth and claw,'" Frank said.

Inside, two EMTs were hoisting the huge body onto a gurney.

By now, Frank had won a few thousand dollars. Bogota walked over to the concession stand. When he returned, he held two plain hotdogs.

"Thank you," I said, reaching for the hotdogs.

"Not for you," he said, retracting his hand.

At the end of the fourth, we skipped betting on the race and walked outside. Frank went to the Chevy and opened the trunk. He removed a gym bag that was nearly bursting. Bogota opened his duffel bag and pulled out a pistol which he placed in his beltline behind his back. He took out a long metal pipe and stuffed it inside his jacket. His hair was matted with sweat.

"I look like shit," he said to Frank.

"You're gorgeous."

Frank led us around the track and toward that row of old shotgun shacks. Bogota was still holding the hotdogs. Frank handed Bogota a plastic bag with big white pills. He threw the buns of the hotdogs into the grass and began to stuff the pills into small pieces of hotdog. We marched past the tall palm trees. The dogs were yelping inside. The heat was immense. Frank stepped up to one of the Mexican trainers and handed him a wad of bills. He did a quick count, gave him a "Si, senor." With the money in hand, they all conveniently decided to take a break.

We were alone now. Two security officers were turning a blind eye to us as well.

Frank looked up the tenth race and found a dog named Hermes' Sandals.

"He's not scratched. So, this is it."

"Maybe you don't need to do this," Bogota said.

"It's not just me that's involved," Frank said.

"Fine," Bogota said.

Frank opened the door to the kennel and stepped inside with Bogota.

"Wait here," Frank said to Bogota and me. Bogota handed him the metal pipe. "Whistle if you see anything unusual."

The dogs were penned, and rows of cages lined both sides of the building. The stink of urine putrefied the air with an acidity that bordered on electricity. Bogota scanned his eyes back and forth across the lot. I heard the announcer call the official results of the last race. I looked at the tickets in my hand again.

"We won again," I said, "not all three, but we won."

"Yippee."

Frank had been in there longer than expected and Bogota was restless. "Wait here," he said. "I'm serious." He disappeared into the stink of the kennel. I grew bored outside, and the infernal Florida sun was melting me. I opened the door and entered. Inside the kennel, the dogs went mad. I walked past a row of cages and now I could see Frank and Bogota. Bogota's hands were on his hips, and he looked impatient. Frank's head was down. He was holding that piece of a long, metal pipe.

"Frank, we've got to go," he whispered. "Post is in fifteen minutes. Get it done."

"I just thought it would be easier."

The door to the pen was open, and a dog skipped around Frank, wagging his tail and licking at his hand. A piece of masking tape was on the top of the cage. It said "Hermes' Sandals."

The dog was out of his pen and walking around them in circles and jumping and barking, waiting for affection. Frank grabbed the dog by the collar, and it let out a surprised yelp. Frank drew the syringe from his pocket and injected the black dog in the shoulder. The dog yelped and then shrank away from him.

Bogota looked at the names on the other cages. When he found the names of the dogs that he was looking for, he released them also. He held out his hand as if offering holy host. They came to him immediately and took the pieces of hotdogs.

"This one and this one," he said pointing to the two dogs. He pet the top of one of their heads. "Get it done," he said to Frank.

The other two dogs were bouncing about, hoping for another piece of the hotdog. Bogota looked to Frank to get the job done. Frank grabbed the dog by the collar. He held him still, took aim, and wound up his arm with the pipe.

The universe had aligned into a singular light, but there were no halos. Only, Frank, abandoned to himself, impotent. He still held the dog by the collar, and he lifted the pipe again and again, but failed to deliver. The dog simply followed the movement of his hand, oblivious to any threat maybe feeling as though Frank was going to play a game of catch.

He bowed his head. "I'm sorry," Frank said.

"You have to get it done. We are running out of time," Bogota said calmly.

The air evacuated from the building, leaving only the suffocating, stained heat.

"I thought that it would be easier," Frank said. He was paralyzed by his intuition. He lifted the pipe. "I. I just can't, man. I can't do it." The pipe fell to the floor with a loud clanking reverberation. Frank took a few steps back and leaned against a desk. He didn't look up.

Bogota snatched the pipe from the ground, and in the same motion grabbed the one dog by the collar that he was just petting the moment before and held him still with his gigantic hand. He looked at Frank and me and shook his head. He wound up and cracked the dog in the shin with the pipe. The clink against the bone was an unnatural sound. The dog howled and shrank away from him, limping away and hopping from his bruised leg. It was not broken, but badly damaged. The dog cringed and let out a heart-wrenching cry that spoke more of betrayal than pain. Bogota dragged the other terrified dog out of the cage and gave him the same treatment. He administered the pipe to both of his legs in a systematic way and placed him back into the cage. The penned dogs were driven to insanity. The injured dogs were whining in pain. Frank covered his ears to escape the whimpering in the cage. He slumped down into the chair now.

Bogota slammed the cage doors closed. He grabbed Hermes' Sandals and forced him back into his cage.

"It's done," Bogota said. He tucked the pipe back in his belt. "Let's go."

He walked over to the desk and hovered over Frank. He pulled the pipe from his belt.

"I'd like to fucking use this on you." Then he suddenly turned on me. "I thought I fucking told you to wait outside. Are you deaf?"

"I'm sorry."

"I asked you a question, boy. Are you deaf?"

Tears were streaming from his eyes. A low and pitiful whine came from the cage. Bogota sat down. He covered his ears. He screamed. Frank stared absently into space. His eyes empty and unflinching.

FOUR MEN WERE gathered near the fence line of the dog track dressed in Bermuda shorts and tropical shirts. They wouldn't have seemed much different than everyone else except that they were watching us and not the races.

"Looks like the old gang is here," Bogota said. He was not looking at Frank. His face was red, and he was sweating.

"Yup," Frank nodded toward the fence line. "Think they are here for me?"

"No Frank," Bogota said. "They're just big fans of the food here," he said tossing half of his excuse for a hamburger into the garbage.

"Ok then, I'll be back shortly."

Frank went to make a bet. He couldn't help himself. He went to a private room with the duffel bag. He was in. Full boat. The Bermuda shorts men never took their eyes from me.

I could forgive Frank for not striking the dog, but not for conjuring the idea. I could forgive him for his past but not the very clear deduction that he had dug his way out of life with cheap, self-serving acts of violence.

Had Frank murdered a man for the same reason? Or did he have Bogota save his ass again? I felt revulsion for him. If he was going to deliver the blow, if he was going to save himself, he should have had the stones to do it himself. What was Bogota but his dutiful dog, mopping up the messes, cleaning up the shit? I wanted to see where the story would end.

"You said that I could learn more at a dog track than I could in any university," I said.

"And have you?" Frank asked.

"Yes," I said.

Frank was studying his program.

"This is what you do?"

"What's that?"

"You said that you would tell me what you do when you are doing it, and this is what you do."

Frank did not answer.

"There is no beauty in this."

Hermes' Sandals was originally going off at 30:1. By the time Frank had returned, the odds dropped dramatically. It was ten minutes to post.

"I'm through, Frank," Bogota said.

Post time was in five minutes. The dogs were on the track and being led to the starting line. Hermes' Sandals was clearly agitated. The Bermuda shorts crowd looked from us to the starting gate and back again. Frank was sitting in one of bandstand chairs. Bogota stood. He had to wear the jacket to hide the pistol.

"It's the same old story."

"Quiet. I'm busy sending good mojo."

"It's just the same boring story. I have to go…"

"You don't have to go anywhere."

"Let me finish," Bogota said. "I have to go. I don't have a choice. But you. You choose this."

"Do we have to do this now?"

"If you are wrong, this ends with them killing you, Frank."

Frank looked down at his notes.

"It doesn't matter who your father is. It doesn't matter that you brought the son of a cop as a bargaining chip when those other ones you think you hold go down," Bogota said. "Which they inevitably will do."

Frank slammed down the notebook and stood up, and it looked as though he was about to take a swing at Bogota. Bogota put both of his hands in his pockets and stuck his perfectly crafted chin out. "Do what you gotta do, Frank."

"Is that what you think?" Frank's face was inches from Bogota. He never broke his stare. The dogs were brought to the starting line. "Race is about to start," Frank whispered, and he turned toward the track.

Silence came over the crowd. The bell rang. The rabbit was released. Hermes' Sandals burst from the door and took an easy five lengths. Frank chewed on his hand.

"Frank, do you know what happens if the dog catches the rabbit?"

"I know goddamn well what happens."

"What happens if he catches the rabbit?" I asked.

"It's not the briar patch," Bogota said.

The Bermuda shorts men used their binoculars to follow the progress of the race. It was only seconds, but it seemed as though the race had fallen into slow motion. Even at a distance, Hermes' Sandals looked like a sure win. He was rounding the final length. The bandaged number five was a far second. Hermes' Sandals was coming down the final stretch with an easy win. Frank was out of his seat, yelling "Go! Go!"

"Can you answer me?" Bogota asked. "'Out brief candle.'"

There was no photo finish. It was a clear and decisive win.

"We need to go. Now," Frank said.

Two of the Bermuda shorts men had separated from the group and were fanning out toward us. Near the far exit past the grand-stand, a trainer was talking with one of the security officers and pointing in Frank's direction.

"We need to scoot. Now!" Frank said.

"What about the winnings?" Bogota asked.

He handed the ticket to Bogota with the winning payoff.

"No time now," Frank said. "We'll come back and cash in." He turned his head side to side. "Anything?"

We took the escalator downstairs and mingled in with the crowd that was leaving.

"Good for now," Bogota said. "But that shouldn't last too long."

"What did you do Frank?"

"We gotta go."

Bogota checked the back of his pants to make sure the gun was in place.

"How much did you lose?"

Frank craned his neck, slowly panning the moving space. He spoke softly, not breaking from his scan.

"I won."

THE AIR IN the bus station was stale even when it was cycled through several stand-up fans. An old woman with a plaid traveling bag sat alone in the rows of orange seats. Bogota bought a ticket to Orlando from a pimply kid with an old grey and white striped conductor's hat. In Orlando, he would transfer to a train and be back in Jersey by the next morning. I couldn't imagine how he would fit into just one of the bus seats.

"You won Frank. It's over."

Frank was up and looking at some old and uninteresting paintings in the bus terminal.

"Where did you get the tip anyway? How are they tied to this?"

Frank paced up and down the lobby. He kept looking outside at the parking lot.

"I didn't," Frank said.

"Then what were they doing there?"

"That was a pretty shitty thing that you said to me."

"Knock off the bullthrow, Frank. Your feelings are of no concern to me right now."

"There was no tip. They're collecting on a mark that I got out of New York."

Bogota was stunned. He covered his face with his huge hands. "There was no tip? You risked it on a hunch."

"And a mark that I took in Las Vegas."

"Christ, Frank. What kind of numbers are we talking?"

"And Chicago."

"I would have never let you risk that. You lied to me Frank. And, you lied to him," Bogota stood and paced past the rows of orange seats. "I've had a lifetime of you. There is no science in this, no bright and beautiful algorithms. It's a beast Frank. And it is devouring you."

"It wasn't a hunch. It's what I do. I studied its history. I did the work. And, in the end it was the name that made sense."

"Hermes' Sandals?"

"Yes."

"What the fuck does that have to do with anything?"

Overhead, the conductor was announcing arrivals and departures.

"So, pay them. Why are we on the run?"

"No."

"What do you mean, no? How much?"

"An elephant's ass," Frank said.

"What the hell does that mean?"

"High and stinky."

Frank, pay them. Or they *will* kill you. You know this."

"They owe me."

"They owe you?"

Frank fingered the contours of the artwork, tracing his finger over the shapes.

"Ten years, Jerome."

Bogota's demeanor changed, softened. He walked towards Frank, reaching for his shoulder. "Frank…"

Frank sensed Bogota's presence and quickly moved to the side, to the next painting, waving with his hand like a player who sends the medical staff back to the sideline after getting knocked down. "I know how this business is handled," Bogota said. "And the reason that I know is because I was the one who would handle it."

"I aim to collect every last shilling, every goddamn ruble, every farthing," Frank said, "And every dollar."

"He should come with me," Bogota said pointing at me.

"I know that he should."

The announcer called the arrival of Bogota's bus.

Frank and Bogota looked at one another and at their thirty years of shared history. I stepped forward to hug him. He backed away from me before I could touch him, turned and walked out to the bus.

40

"DO YOU WANT to drive?" Frank asked me.
Stepping into the driver's seat of the Chevy was strange.
I eased into the cracked leather seat that seemed perfectly contoured just for Frank. The grip of the steering wheel was unfamiliar, like walking into someone's home when they are gone. I turned the key and the car yielded with a growl of the engine. Alligator Alley was a straight shot across Florida. Frank put his feet out the window. The heat was building, even in the early morning.

"Why did Bogota leave?" I asked. Frank brought his feet back in the car. He folded his hands between his legs and stared at the open and lonely road. The wind had shifted and brought strong gusts though the open windows. Frank rolled up his window and I did the same.

"Atoms make up molecules. Molecules form covalent bonds. Those bonds carry the most fundamental and delicate balance of attraction and repulsion. Opposites. Covalent Bonds shoulder the burden of nothingness in order to exist. And they do exist. Silent, unseen. And Beautiful."

The Chevy relaxed beneath my hands like a horse that had been broken. The car and its motion were fluid now, and it eased though the gears, and no longer bucked against my shifting.

"Even at our most elemental, Brogan, we dance."

I sped the car up and passed a stranded driver on the side of the road. He was waving his hands at us like some kind of schizoid.

208

"Keep going," Frank said.

We sped past him. I could see the man in the rearview mirror, giving us the middle finger. We should have stopped and helped him. Nature is red in tooth and claw.

"And you never dance alone," Frank said. "It doesn't take much to break a molecule. To break water into hydrogen and oxygen, you need simply to add heat."

I shook my head. More riddles more science. "How – in any way – does this answer my question? Why is it so difficult for you to give me a simple answer?"

"The answers are always in front of you. You just need to look more closely for them. "

A police car with its sirens on was catching up quickly behind us. With everyone chasing us now, it seemed that he was after us also. I pulled to the side praying that he would pass. Praying that whatever was in the trunk wouldn't land us in jail.

"Are we in trouble?"

"Yes. But not both of us."

"I think I'm scared."

"Look closer."

"What?"

"I'm not."

After the police car passed, I pulled the Chevy back onto the highway. It was Sunday, and as of 3:08 A.M., I was eighteen years old. The moment had passed without any magical transition. No threshold had been crossed. No line had been crossed. It simply happened, unnoticed. Florida rolled by as endless miles of odd birds and reptiles and swamp land. To the south, black thunderheads were forming. In the distance, past the wasted and barren landscape, suddenly civilization began to appear on the horizon.

"Who were those men at the track?" I asked.

"Insurance policies."

"Are they gangsters?"

"You've probably watched too many movies."

"No Frank. I haven't."

"They were more like businessmen."

The road was a long straight-away to the east coast. Frank did not play his music. There was only the wind. Frank would go in and out in a sleepy daze. I could only think, replay the scenarios, formulate theories.

"What did you think of Diane?" Frank asked, suddenly awake now. "Did she remind you of anything?"

"Really Frank," I said. "What difference does it make?"

"We met at a bar in Old San Juan. She would always sing this song for me about a guy who drinks gin, fucks off, and always comes home late or doesn't come home at all. I suppose I always related to it. That's my kind of song. God, I adored her for that, but not in a lover's way, just friendship. I had a reputation by then for madness. By the way, I'm okay with that. No need to hide from the family fare. I think she liked that sort of thing. She had these crazy green eyes that stared at mine a bit too long."

Everything made me jumpy. Every car that was behind us. Every mile that we drove to wherever we were going. Frank was not scared. He didn't worry about it. He wanted to tell his story.

"Sweetest, green-eyed, most beautiful, most perfect thing that I had ever seen. I wonder whether I have concocted my own perfect memory of that time. Others might tell it a different way. But that is the way it goes, Brogan. Love simply, Brogan. Then you will have no regrets. It really is all that we have."

He dipped his head low and closed his eyes again.

"I didn't know that she was pregnant when she left," he said.

"Then why did she leave?"

"A bit of heat breaks the bond."

41

NTERSTATE I-95 WELCOMED us back again, and we headed
farther south. Frank eventually woke up and directed me to stop
at a liquor store. A mile down the highway, the bones of an old
roller coaster rose from the east alongside a big Ferris wheel and
the flickering lights of a carnival.

"Get off the highway," Frank said.

We took the exit and circled around to a large open field that
was lined with cars. A parking attendant was directing us, and
children were running toward the rides and toward the sweet smell
of popcorn and cotton candy. A golden cardboard gate was painted
to look like giant doors. Two guards in medieval costumes and
tennis shoes handed out flyers and directed the crowds.

"Are we getting out?"

"It's your birthday," Frank said. "Not exactly Disneyland but
fuck it."

We paid our admission and walked into the festival. We played
the ring toss and the prize wheel. Carnival booths sold large and
small beers. Frank drank the large ones. The fair was trashy, worn
out, cheap. It was magnificent.

Frank bought tickets for the rides. We waited in a long line for the
roller coaster. The cars rolled up to the attendant. The old group filed
out, and we took our place at the back of the car. The cars climbed up
the steep slope, with a click, click, click, like a countdown. The cars

dipped over the horizon, dragging us headlong into a spectacular plunge. The children screamed. We descended, and Frank opened his arms to the sunlight. He flung his head back and laughed out loud. He let the momentum of the car whip him from side to side. He guffawed and lost his breath and his chest heaved to find its rhythm again. The other passengers risked a strained neck to poke a look at him. We dove into twists, and the car rocked us from side to side. His eyes were closed.

When the ride stopped, Frank remained in his seat. A new group of passengers was ready to board, but he did not move. I went to get up.

"Stay put, Brogan."

"Show's over," the attendant said.

"We're going again, Sport," Frank said.

"You can get back in line."

"I don't think that will be necessary," Frank said.

Frank's beer-tinged smile bared his teeth. He gave the attendant another two tickets, and a folded one-hundred-dollar bill. The attendant took it in his hand and turned it over, obviously confused.

"Just us this time. Solo trip, you dig it?" Frank said.

The line was long to get back on the ride. The attendant held the two tickets and the money. The crowd was angry. He sneaked a glance at Frank once more.

"I'm sorry. You have to wait back in the line," he said trying to hand the money back to Frank.

"Not necessary," Frank said.

"Let's go," Someone screamed from the line of people.

Frank wasn't moving. The ticket-taker halted the line, leaving Frank and I alone on the ride. He motioned to the conductor to start the ride again. The conductor gave him a confused look. He was scared. "Just go again," he said nervously to the booth. "Please." As we climbed the steep slope to the drop, I could hear the jeers of a furious crowd.

"Fuck them, Brogan. It is your birthday."

We exited the ride, past the catcalls and boos of the still angry line. Beneath the shadows of the trestles of the ride, a sea of children surrounded Frank. They were chanting a nursery rhyme that was a soothing, repetitive lullaby. They interlocked hands and spun in a circle.

The chant became louder and faster. Frank was a ridiculous giant among them. He caught onto the tune and chimed in, singing to the sky.

Their motion was like a great electromagnetic conductor, speeding its revolution and producing a massive jolt of electricity. Frank held his hands out and spun around.

"Ring around the Rosie!"

Frank began to dance. Not the same dance that he danced with Diane, but a Shamanic-like, Indian dance. He shook his hands loose, beat his head up and down, breathed a fiery breath, sucked in the universe, drew light into himself. He beat with his legs to a rhythm that only he could hear.

"Pocket full of posies."

The children watched him, and he encouraged them to continue. His dance moved to their music and cadence, yet was strangely outside of it, beyond it, and disposed of it.

The parents, hearing the growing volume of the song were drawn back to the circle of children. They laughed with nervous eyes.

"Ashes to ashes! We all fall down."

The children were now being forcibly taken from the circle by the parents, grabbing their hands, breaking that chain of voices until there was no longer sound.

Frank continued to spin, already infused with that energy. Frank kept the rhythm until he lost his balance and collapsed onto the ground.

He burped his beer and re-varnished all with that incendiary laughter that cackled of flint on stone, a cry and a laugh, a match to gasoline.

"We all fall down," Frank said.

The children were laughing. The parents were frightened.

A woman with a plaid skirt and white polo broke from her husband and their young daughter and approached Frank with caution. "I think that it would be best if you leave."

Frank stood up, steadied himself, and then walked past the man toward the ice cream stand. He pulled a twenty-dollar bill from his pocket.

"Buy all these little bastards an ice cream," he said.

The young girl serving the ice cream was confused. She hesitated and looked at the crowd of nervous parents.

"It's his birthday," he said pointing to me. "Just do it."

"I thought you hated kids?" I asked.

He smiled.

Frank was dancing his way to the car still singing the nursery rhyme. He was flushed from the beer. He ducked his head into his hands as the sun set. He was laughing an uncontrollable laugh, but nothing seemed that funny. He looked at me, tears streaming through the laughter, and the bloody mess of his cracked eyes.

FRANK WAS READY for another six-pack. We stopped at a gas station in Fort Lauderdale, and he bought beer and potato chips, and a new t-shirt for me that said, "Fort Lauderdale Spring Break 1989".

We continued south, drinking beer and listening to the radio. The traffic in Miami was backed up to the causeway and Frank just became drunker and drunker. We stopped when he ran out of alcohol. We broke through the mess of sports cars and tractor trailers and Cuban jalopies. We picked up even more beer, and I drank one with Frank.

I was his beer man.

I wouldn't let him down. When we reached the Florida Keys, it seemed like the end of the world. Frank pulled into a strip mall. The stores were closed and dark and the parking lot was empty. I eased the Chevy between the narrow white lines. Frank was fast asleep. I watched the descending moon in the bright and open sky descending like a lone lantern.

The next morning, when we awoke, I squinted at the sunlight. The trees were a chorus of tropical birds. My head was pounding. Frank was awake. The stores of the strip mall were alive and awake.

"I didn't want to wake you," he said.

"I'm fine, thanks."

"This is it now. No more tilting at windmills."

"What's *it*?"

"The *denouement*."

He was chewing on his hand. Frank smiled and I couldn't tell if he was a smile of satisfaction or a slow slide to madness. He started the Chevy, and we were off again. Not far into the trip, he stopped at a roadside shanty, changed in some dollars and made a few phone calls. I wondered how far Bogota had made it. I wondered what it was like to know impending death. I couldn't take the loneliness that he must have felt. I wondered what would become of us at the fringe of the continent.

The rural, sandy towns gave way to Key West, a town bustling in purples and tropical greens. It was a paradise of outsiders. In the early afternoon traffic, we crawled by the plantation-type homes with the huge porches and thin balustrades and wide supporting pillars. We parked and walked around the town like tourists. Frank stepped into one of the many of plentiful bars and bought colorful drinks in tall plastic glasses that were laden with rum.

As the day came to an end, we returned to the car and finished the last of the beer. I was starting to feel sick. We walked to Mallory Square. The crowd was hushed, and the sun was setting.

"This isn't the way that I planned this," Frank said.

"There was a plan?" I asked.

He laughed and took a nip of a small bottle of bourbon. I knew that look now; the mask removed. He was plastered once again.

"I was hoping for an illumination. An epiphany," Frank said.

Frank's language reminded me that he was a mad addict, scratching away at a never healing scar. But, even in his most impulsive scramble, it felt to me like he was trying to accomplish something, something there, but not there, just out of reach.

When Will would sometimes have me attend AA Meetings with him, people would talk about these moments. Times when they knew they had gone too far; that they knew they should change their lives. These were moments that made people take stock in themselves and realize that their addictions fueled their dishonesty, self-loathing, or hurt.

"When we tell our own stories with conviction," Frank said, pointing his finger authoritatively at nothing, "what's funny is that we always think we are right, that what we are saying is really the truth."

We sat near the wall and watched a street performer. A man was leading a little dog along a high wire with a small crowd in a semi-circle around him. Another character was juggling fire. A woman was telling fortunes. The sun was about to set, the real show.

"My real father was a real punter. And by that, I mean a professional gambler and card player of the highest order. The kind who gives marks. And lives well."

"Who...."

"They called him Vinny the Legs. Some people said it was because of his skinny chicken strips that kept him strutting. Others said it was because he would have yours cut off if you crossed him."

A large crowd had gathered in Mallory square. The pier jutted far out into the Gulf of Mexico, like one long finger pointing west. The sun was setting in a fan of pinks and deep serpentine red lines. Men fished from the pier. In the glinting last of the sunlight, they pulled fish from the ocean. The waves lapped against the legs of the pier in a thousand babbling voices. We walked all the way to the end, parting the crowds until we found a comfortable spot at the end. The clouds were breaking apart, and shapes emerged from nothingness.

"The Funkie was scared shitless of him. I didn't blame him for that. Most people were." Frank heaved a deep sigh. "I do blame him for taking everything out on me."

The sun now dipped below the horizon, and the crowd let out a cheer. We walked back towards the Chevy. It looked sinister and out of place beneath the palm trees and the coral greens and the bright yellows of Key West.

"Mr. Vincent also knew horses. Intuitively. Like no one I've ever seen – a sixth sense."

"Who?"

"Vinny the Legs."

"Why did you call him that? Mr. Vincent?"

"Dad never worked for me."

"Dad?"

"Doesn't sound right, does it? 'The sins of the father are visited on the son.'"

Frank opened the trunk. Two huge bundles containing tightly wrapped one hundred dollar bills sat in the well in place of a tire.

"That is what you have been betting with?" I asked.

"Yes," he said and closed the trunk and locked it. "And no."

FRANK LED US to a pub on a narrow street with stools on the outside of a half-moon bar and an open patio. The news was airing sports highlights. His hands shook. He chewed the bottom of his palms and gnawed on his nails. An hour ago, we were bathed in that spectacular sunlight of Florida. We were now in a hellish darkness.

"Do you know when my birthday is?" Frank asked.

"No," I said.

"October 25," Frank said. "Upon St. Crispin's day!"

"I won't forget it."

"I'm sending you back."

"Why?"

Frank ordered two drinks. He handed one to me.

"Here. Tits and tonsils."

"What are you going to do with the money?"

Frank exhaled a satisfied groan after his drink. "I got plans for it."

"Is this what Bogota was talking about? When he said they would kill you?"

He stole another glance at the television, and this time, he just chuckled.

"Never happen."

He dismissed any continuation in that conversation.

"I got a good line on a few games tomorrow, though." He stopped speaking suddenly and stared at his cigarettes for a long time. He packed the box slowly and deliberately before pulling on one. "Remember what I told you. Try to remember all the important things that I have been saying to you. Don't ever welch on a bet. Be smart. Think before you speak. Never lend or borrow money. Clothes make the man. Accidents make people."

He smiled and shook as if he was laughing, but it was uneasy, more like a gag or convulsion that someone has when a foreign body enters their body.

He took a long, slow drag, then turned back to me.

"Most of all, don't do what I do."

Frank walked to an upright piano near the window. He played a few chords.

"What about stealing?'

"It's not like that Brogan," he said. "The servant went to the master to beg forgiveness for his debt."

He continued playing. He was quite good, but he stopped often and flexed his bad hand. He played a few off keys and stopped again.

"And for that – I served ten years."

It began to sink in. The long absence.

"For what…"

He practiced a few more chords on the piano once more and looked up at a crowd of people that entered the bar. Frank continued to play and shook his head.

"Murder? You killed someone?" I asked, remembering the stories at Thanksgiving.

Frank smiled. "You could say that. They did. In my silent retort and subsequent incarceration, the master was satisfied."

The game on the television came to an end

"Until now, it seems."

"So, all that nonsense about borrowing and lending and never welching on a bet – that was all bullshit?"

Frank shrugged his shoulders and reached for a light. "Hey – no shit, no roses."

Frank scanned his eyes across the bar, and I followed his gaze.

"Inevitably, Brogan, we fall. But, for a brief second – suspended in the air, springing from the cliffs – we are perfect. Waves of energy held together by the dance. Enjoy the flow and rhythm, and in the end, just be happy where you end up."

Frank gave me a hard pat on the back.

"Enjoy the ride, my son."

A gorgeous woman skated by us. "Brogan, look at the goddamn legs on that one. I mean for Christ's sake, just look at those stems."

I put my hand on his shoulder. "Frank, can I ask you a question?"

"You just did," he said and laughed.

"You said that when you left Puerto Rico that you didn't know Diane was pregnant."

"I didn't know," he said.

"Did you ever find out what happened?"

"Yes," he said.

Outside, I could see that a festival had started on the streets with fireworks. A parade of drag queens was dancing down the street. Frank needled the keys of the piano.

Frank stopped playing and stared down at the piano keys. "You really are a smart kid. Now that you have the answers, I'll have a Maker's Mark, neat," he said turning and yelling to the bartender. "And he'll have the same."

THE BARTENDER RETURNED with two glasses of the brown liquid. I took a sip and tasted that awful gasoline taste, that searing fire, and I fell into a fit of coughing and gagging. We stared into a mirror that was behind the piano. Frank's reflection and the uncanny resemblance. Who do we trust the most? Who is that one person that you can rely on to give it to you straight? Frank had Bogota. Bogota was gone now. I had Dan, and Dan was long dead. Will and Linda had told me a lie. I knew the truth, and the truth was the artichoke.

"I used to go to meet Mr. Vincent on Sundays. That's how I learned how to play. He taught me." Frank began to play what sounded like an old jazz melody. "I used to love doing this." He played a few classical notes. He missed a note with the missing tip of his fingers and then he stopped playing. "I think that's why The Funkie fucked up my hand. He never wanted me to play. It reminded him that he wasn't my father."

Across the bar, a man with a Puerto Rican flag on his jacket was speaking Spanish. He was joined by a tall man with terribly pocked, Cracker Jack skin, and another wearing a patch of the Puerto Rican flag on his shoulder. They never looked away from us. The Puerto Rican man fidgeted against the bar and snorted back tequila shots. His knuckled hand dipped into his jacket and found a pack of cigarettes nestled next to the butt end of a pistol.

"That man has a gun," I said to Frank.

"Yes, he does," Frank said. Frank grabbed me by the shirt and pulled me close. "The moon and the stars, kid" Frank said to me. "They are yours now, and your decisions will be your own from now on. There are no stones unturned. Make your own decisions."

He let go of my shirt and stared at the man across the bar. Outside, the festival continued. The finale of fireworks was exploding in the air above us, detonating, blasts, and bright beautiful streaks like colorful tears. The fireworks display ended, and the crowd broke into a manic applause.

The last few notes dwindled down into the vibrating wires of the piano and hung on the air. Frank closed the casing over the piano keys, and we walked back to the bar and took our same two seats. This was what he wanted.

"Buy those assholes a tequila," he said to the bartender and nodded toward the Puerto Rican men.

The two men looked up when the drinks arrived. They pushed the two shots back toward the bartender.

I saw Frank's future. I had knowledge now.

"I just wanted to get this right," Frank said.

"I know, Frank."

My stomach felt like Mt Vesuvius.

"You don't see that too often in this life. People getting it right. Just once."

You see, you can place your bet now, and stack up the odds in your favor. College, a degree, a good job. But remember this, if you take the safe bet and lose, life is going to smack you in the ass with a pretty hefty vig.

This was the vig. The juice. The kick in the ass.

The bourbon, the whirlwind of the past couple of days, the lack of sleep, the confusion, they rose up in my stomach. I nearly knocked the stool over running to the bathroom. Before I entered the bathroom, I barely contained my composure before the inevitable eruption of vomit. I leaned against the wall to steady myself. Frank caught my eye. He looked at me for a long time, nodded his head and turned away. He faded back into the blurry patterns of the room, dissolving into the darkness and light at once.

I barely made it into the bathroom stall and before I had the seat of the toilet bowl raised, I retched with such ferocity that the puke splattered a mural across the wall. I dry heaved everything that I had in my soul.

I had to get back out there. I felt it in the air.

I could hear the bathroom door opening, and the muffled voices from the bar. The cool of the porcelain was soothing. I wanted to find Frank, but the room spun around, and my feet wouldn't work. I could hear footsteps on the tile. The door closed and now it was quiet. The stall door next to me opened and closed. I could hear the tapping of shoes against the tile floor. My door opened.

I continued to throw up. It came in waves and spasms, shooting and burning out of my nose. When I was able to look up, I could see the deep pockmarks of his skin, the gnarled hands and the scars. He started to reach for me.

A pistol suddenly appeared at the man's temple, and he froze.

"I will kill you," Bogota's voice said. "Believe me when I tell you this. I will kill you and not think a second thought about it. Back away, and out the door, and you may see manana," Bogota said.

Then there was a hand on my neck, and I was lifted off my feet. I was blind from the tears and the puking.

"Move! Now!" Bogota said. But I couldn't move. "Up!" he said. He put me behind his enormous mass, and we backed out of the door. "Hands on top of your head," he said to the Cracker Jack man. "On your knees and turn around." The Puerto Rican man got down on his knees. He began to place his hands on his head, but before he could finish, Bogota turned the gun around and slammed the butt of the gun against the man's temple. Cracker Jack collapsed into the stall. His head cracked horribly on the toilet.

"Move. Now!" Bogota said.

He still had me by the back of my shirt and dragged me outside of the bathroom. To avoid the bar, he kicked opened the door to the kitchen. The staff was stunned and looked up in terror at Bogota. He found the exit, and we were in an alley behind the bar. The stench of the restaurant garbage was overwhelming, and I retched again. He was holding me up with one hand and peering around the corner.

"Let's go. Move it!" he said.

"Frank?"

When we got to the Chevy, Bogota threw me in the front seat and closed the door. The trunk groaned open. I coughed and wiped my eyes.

"Is he really, you know, my father?"

The inside of the car shook from the force with which Bogota closed the door of the trunk. And, then there was darkness.

I **AWOKE ONCE SOMEWHERE** in the vast wasteland of Florida and found that I was asleep on Bogota's chest. We were parked in the usual rest stops. His hand still held the pistol. Outside, the regular world went on without a heartbeat missed, with people coming and going from the roadside restaurants, with all the world in motion, oblivious, and not giving a good goddamn about any of it.

"I have to know if it is the truth."

"Sleep now," Bogota said.

When we reached Miami airport, Bogota collected my things and walked me to the gate. He bought me a ticket for Newark, New Jersey. We waited in the airport restaurant. Bogota ordered us peaches with whip cream, and we watched the world outside the giant windows.

"I had a lot of time to think."

Bogota talked with his mouth full. He closed his eyes and seemed to savor the peaches.

"When I understood. When I knew the true trouble that he was in, I knew I had to turn around."

He coughed and pitched forward and fought to catch his breath. Blood had collected around his mouth. He wiped the blood away. He ran one finger around the top of the bowl and gathered the whip cream.

"You were born in New Jersey. Not Puerto Rico. You may not know this, but I was the first person to hold you," he said.

When he finished the last of the peaches, he leaned his gigantic arms on the table. He dipped his head down and thought for a long time.

"I called you 'the little old man.' You didn't cry. You just looked around the room. Eyes wide open. Diane was in labor for only a short time, as if you couldn't wait to get out."

The crowded airport faded away, the bustle, the overhead announcements, the voices silenced, and only Bogota was there.

"Will came to the hospital in the middle of his midnight shift. I can still remember him in that blue uniform and the shining badge. Linda was already there also."

Bogota looked over my shoulder. He ran his eyes back and forth as if he was looking for something. I turned around once, and only saw the nameless travelers hustling through the airport. I looked back at him. Silent. Hoping that he would continue.

"I held you first and then handed you to Diane, who then handed you over to Linda. Linda couldn't have children. They knew that from the start."

He leaned back again and threw his huge arms into the air. It took me some time to process what he just said. I thought of all of them in the same room at one time, younger, confused versions, almost kids themselves.

Bogota grabbed the keys off the table and stuffed them into his jacket. He ran a hand through his thick black hair and pushed it back from his forehead.

"They couldn't take you with them, Brogan. You have to understand. One was a wanted man. The other was an alcoholic."

Bogota looked over my shoulder again. He was fixed on something behind me. He took the jacket from the back of the chair and put it on.

"You can't blame him for wanting to meet you. You can't blame Will for letting him take you."

Bogota nodded his head at whoever was behind me. He looked directly into my eyes for a long time. A wave of sadness steeled over him. He stood and walked over to me and put his hand on my shoulder.

"Any one of us would have killed to have a father and mother that loved us that much."

He turned and walked in the opposite direction fading into the throng of Miami tourists. I turned around to see what Bogota was looking at. Will walked out from the terminal doors. He looked as though he hadn't slept since I left.

LINDA WAS WAITING at Newark Airport when we had landed in New Jersey. She was wearing one of Will's heavy flannel shirts and a pair of worn jeans. She put her arm around me, and I shrugged her off so violently that she was terrified. She began to cry. Will grabbed me against my protests and held me until I relented.

I slept straight through for two days. Embryo encased in the folds of deep bedding, I was rooted in darkness, static and larval, cocooned and diffident. The winter days passed. I was in and out of dreams. Will would sit at the end of my bed at night. I would wake to the orange glow of his cigarette. I would wake to Linda. She read in my room and stood sentry. She brought grilled cheese sandwiches and warm soup. She placed cold compress towels on my fevered head. I would stare at her. "Think of a dream," she would say and put her hand over my eyes. "A place where you can go."

One morning, I awoke and showered and put on my Seton Prep school jacket. I went downstairs to find a surprised Will and Linda, pausing halfway through coffee. Linda made my favorite meal, French toast. I left without eating.

The snow was gathering on the quad just outside the windows of Seton Prep, and most of the students were gathered in their winter coats and red scarves, throwing snowballs, and running off to the parking lot to their cars, and leaving to gather at the Quick Bite cafe.

The detention hall was light that day with two other students who were working steadily on their essays, blowing snot into rags, falling asleep, and then jerking awake. No monitor was assigned that day, and we were left on our own to finish the required writing. Every twenty minutes Mr. D., one of the high ranking batshits at the Prep, peeked in the room to make sure that no "grabass" was going on.

In and out of the drifts of an overheated winter classroom, I learned that it wasn't a thought of anger or even sadness, or even love. I couldn't feel any of those. Maybe an extended curiosity, or just a longing. M.I.T. seemed like another planet that I would be visiting soon. *Planet Motherfucker.* There were still too many unanswered questions. The idea was to try and define the "it."

I met with several therapists. That was Linda's idea. A professional. "Let the professionals handle it." The therapist said it's like Santa Clause walking around with a huge bag, and that slowly we would begin to pull out each memory like a gift and look at it, turn it over, examine the contents and decide whether it was something we would want to keep. I wanted to punch her in the face. Maybe the number two combination. I had that one down. But how could I reason the mad thoughts and confusion of Frank. *Don't do what I do. Accidents make people.* I was trying to figure what each of these suggestions, combined, meant in the constellation of the universe that to me was Frank. In the end there really wasn't any answer. Just a general acceptance. They didn't know what the "it" was. "It" was like trying to define gravity, as Frank put it. An attraction of an enormous mass that brings everything closer, whether for sustainability or destruction, but in the end, just unexplainable.

"Mr. Camden," Brother Big said.

He had materialized above me, scaring the life out of me as always. I craned my neck upward toward the tremendous figure in a long black robe. Small eyes beneath the glasses. The scent of incense and soap. He was carrying a file beneath his right arm and a bible in the other. He pointed his finger at me and motioned me out of the classroom. On the way out he grabbed one of the students near the front of the classroom, who of course never heard him coming, and shook him until his head almost popped off. "This is not the required assignment," he said holding up the student's loose-leaf paper that was scattered with drawings of girls with huge tits. Along the way, the student was bounced off every locker in the hallway and thrown into the front office.

I placed my backpack on the floor and settled into one of the pews of the chapel.

"'I have gone astray like a lost sheep; seek your servant, for I do not forget your commandments,'" Brother big said in his low and reverberating baritone.

I reached a hand up and touched my eye. The welts from the fist-fight had gone down, but I still had yellowish, blue bruises beneath. I had missed the first few days after the winter break.

"No disrespect to you Brother, but I've had enough of elliptical phrases and quotes to last me a lifetime."

The chapel was quiet. Most of the faculty had left for the day, and the white noise from far off down the corridor was silenced.

"It's on the record that this was an abduction, but we both know the truth about that," he said.

"We both know the truth. And the truth is the artichoke heart. I won't be expelled, and I will be finished here in June and starting M.I.T. in September. So, yes, it was an abduction."

"You left with a black eye, and now you return with a much more pronounced and troubling one."

He was looking directly me, and at the scars on my forehead and the welts and bruises beneath my eyes. "Were you abused?"

"I had a fistfight."

He didn't say anything. "And I went to a strip club."

He breathed a long sigh of frustration. He wasn't angry.

"'I am afraid that when I come again my God will humble me before you, and I will be grieved over many who have sinned earlier and have not repented of the impurity, sexual sin and debauchery in which they have indulged.'"

"It's not like that, Brother."

He loosened the collar around his neck, leaned back in the church pew, and took off his glasses. He ran a hand across his face and small eyes and stared up at the ceiling. The chapel was darkening in the late winter afternoon. Only two small candles illuminated both sides of the tabernacle.

"What are you prepared to do?"

"Serve out the detentions, finish the school year, and start college."

Brother Big shifted in his seat. He secured the bible close to his heart.

"These are mortal stakes, Brogan. Do you understand? The path to self-destruction." His voice was different now. Not the commanding, no-nonsense. It was strained.

I stood up and walked for a bit through the chapel. Brother big folded his hands over his lap and closed his eyes. I walked past the Stations of the Cross, the confessional, the altar. When I returned, he was still in the same position.

"Can I confess something to you?"

"I'm not a priest. I cannot deliver the sacrament of reconciliation."

"Can I tell you anyway?"

He nodded his head yes and stared straight ahead at the altar.

I leaned against the pew facing him. "For as long as I could remember, from when I really started to remember things, Dan Wundt, the best and only friend that I ever had, slides down the hill, a cigarette in his mouth, denim-jacket, dark sunglasses and a Sony Walkman with the earphones on his head." I looked past

Brother Big, and found myself on the front porch of Beechwood Ave. "He is carrying his graffiti spray paint cans. His fingernails are covered in ink. He has a backpack slung over his shoulder, probably carrying something stolen. He is the coolest guy I've ever seen."

We had those silent, unattended, unopened acorns, those seeds of knowledge left untended for fear of what may grow.

Brother Big opened his eyes and stared straight forward.

"Dan always made plans about going somewhere and doing something. He was always telling me about a world that I didn't know. Trips to Los Angeles. Digging up dead rock stars. Music. Girls. Sex."

At this, Brother Big arched an eyebrow, but he let me continue.

"I always had this itch. Like I was missing out. Or, not getting it right. The last words that we ever had were an argument. Dan was always on the wrong road, but I didn't care. I just didn't want him to go down."

Brother Big stood up and leaned on the pew next to me. He folded his arms across his chest.

"He had used duct tape and when he did, he taped his left hand to his left ankle. He had a black blindfold on. There was an unlit cigarette still in his mouth. The lighter had fallen away. His hand was still reaching for it. He used a belt to hang himself. He was long dead when I found him, but I still tried to lift him out of the noose. His body was stiff. He smelled like earth. I left and called the police and waited with the hanging triangle of my friend."

We sat for a long time, and then Brother Big did something that I had never seen him do before. He put an arm around me. We stayed that way in the dark chapel. At least now, I would have something to miss when I left there.

"There was no turning back," I said. "Sometimes you can't stop a horse halfway through the water."

M.I.T. **WAS MUCH** harder than I expected. I wanted to be busy at chasing "that thing between their legs," but my days were full. We talked numbers and talked of abstract ideas. We talked of Chaos Theory and Binary Math. Our professors challenged us to see beyond the symbols, beyond the signals. They wanted us to see math as language, as its own code that spoke to the secrets of the universe's invisible architecture. They talked of Pascal and Kant, then drew a straight line back to Aristotle. I struggled to reconcile the two. Math is. Philosophy aspires to be. I read. I thought. I listened. I was hoping to find an entry point of intersection, of overlap. They didn't seem to jibe. But, even in my studies (as I had come to understand mathematics, and I had studied the properties of covalent bonds, and I had propagated Frank's theory of dogs pissing on trees), when I tried to put two and two together, nothing added up.

It was getting near Thanksgiving. The night before I took the long bus ride back to New Jersey, I walked the river Charles along the banks of the free flowing water with the cold of winter that was more than a thousand miles away, and almost one year from the last night that I saw Frank in Key West. The lights of Boston were warm vestibules to another place, bright skyscrapers that rose quietly above the midnight cityscape, memories that floated in the night sky. They reflected off the water and flowed with the darkness down to remembered places. A lonesome highway on the western coast of Florida, the windows down, the whips of Bogota's long and elegant black hair, the bright gleaming globe of Frank's forehead. And they were laughing. And I am laughing, but I can't quite remember the joke.

48

WAS HOME A day early for Thanksgiving in New Jersey. I searched for a letter, the scent of gasoline.

The phone broke the morning silence. I heard Will coughing, snapping open his cigarette lighter, and then answering the line. A half hour later, a car pulled in front of the house. Two men in sunglasses and black t-shirts jumped from the car and walked to the front door with purpose. I climbed down the stairs and stopped halfway down, giving me a clear view of the front door. My father had the front door cracked open. The chain was still in place. His left arm was behind his back with his un-holstered .45 automatic paused by the side of his leg.

"This was one of the known addresses," The one man said. I can't tell which one is talking. "We just don't want to have to keep coming back here."

"I haven't spoken to him in years," Will said.

"Do you know where he might be?"

"Alaska?" Will said.

"This isn't the time to get funny."

"He has the traveling Jones. What do you want to hear? I haven't seen or spoken to him."

"Ok then," the one man in the black t-shirt, the bigger one stepped up and leaned on the door. Will stepped back into the foyer, he loosened the chain and let the door open, and raised the pistol square between the eyes of the stranger.

"I haven't seen Frank in years," Will said. "And, if you're smart, you won't come around here looking for him."

"You're not being very smart," the other man said with his hands held up on both sides.

"You come to this house again," Will said, "and I will kill you both."

Will closed the door and looked at me on the stairs. We owned an unspoken communication now. He looked outside to make sure that the car had driven off. Linda was awake now. She was in her robe and mussed from her sleep. She looked happy.

The next day, the house was busy with the madness of a Beechwood Avenue Thanksgiving. Uncle George drank his Jack Daniels, and Aunt Margaret stole his glass away from him as often as she could. The cousins and the cousins' kids had grown a year older. Linda was a nut, trying to feed twenty people and trying to make time to talk with everyone. Will watched the football game.

After the turkey and the pie, and the coffee, and the anisette, I sat in the living room and watched the game with my father. He sat on the couch and sipped his decaf coffee. I still had a half of a beer from dinner. When the game had come to a close, I went to the kitchen and helped my mother with the last of the cleanup.

49

THE NIGHT AFTER Thanksgiving was always a big deal in Ridgefield, so I decided to go out. I left Beechwood Ave and walked to the corner local bar, which was welcoming with its bright lights, the bass beat of rock music, and the music of a thousand voices that carried into the cold autumn night.

The pub was tangled with bodies and nice holiday clothes, and smiles. The guys gave hugs and shook hands. The girls came in for an uncomfortable peck on the cheek. We were never really friends, but we had a noticeable love and security just in our familiarity. We noticed in each other's faces how we had changed. Most of my former classmates could legally drink. Not me. Not yet. But on this night the bartenders turned a blind eye, and everyone could drink. I ordered bourbon.

Rich Laforte was seated at a table by himself. He was drinking a beer. He looked different, but still as good looking as ever.

"Brogan," he said and waved a hand at me to join him.

I sat at the table, put down the bourbon, and we stared at one another. He was wearing his U.S. Navy uniform. He had been to war. With the invasion of Kuwait earlier that year, the United States had led a coalition of thirty-five countries in the invasion of Iraq. Last I heard, he was on the initial task force from the start of the campaign.

"How goes? I heard you got kidnapped a couple of years ago."

"That's just a rumor," I said.

"Yeah," he said. "There's always a lot of that around here," he said sweeping a hand across the room.

"How about you?" I asked.

He drank his beer. He had a bit of strange twitch now. "Wasn't what I signed up for. I was just looking for free tuition."

"I'm sorry," I said. "But I know what you mean."

"One minute I'm banging Polynesian chicks, the next we are at war, watching Tomahawk missiles decimate a country." He stared out the window, and I imagine he saw those rockets taking flight, hurtling in the air on a singular purpose. "It's a strange thing, war."

He was on leave and due to return to the battle in the Persian Gulf.

We didn't have much to say to one another after that, but I suppose we had shared some secret agreement not to be assholes to one another. After all, the world had moved on.

"Good to see you, Rich," I said.

"I'll see ya, Brogan."

I left him to his beer. He was alone most of the time. Some of the Veterans from town stopped by and shook his hand. He tried to be cordial. I imagine, like me, he just wanted things to be the same again.

I shook more hands and kissed more cheeks.

Andrea was in a circle of neighborhood girls, sipping on a pinkish martini. She caught my eye and held it. We met at the corner of the bar next to a picture window that let out onto the street. I could see where the alcohol had made its mark with the roundness of her face. I guessed that she now shared her mother's affinity toward Chardonnay.

"Is Rich OK?" I asked.

She smiled and stared down at her drink and didn't answer my question.

"I'm sorry that I never got in touch with you," she said. "I wanted to. There were so many strange rumors."

"That's ok," I said. I sipped my drink. I no longer felt as naked and exposed as when we were kids. I knew too much now.

"I'm sorry for what happened to you."

"It's ok."

She asked about Boston and school, and I ran through the checklist that I gave everyone about the tough classes, and the cold weather. It was vanilla and boring, and I really just didn't know what I wanted to say to her, or even what she wanted to hear.

"I still remember when you called me," she said. "I still remember your poem."

Bogota's poem.

I shrugged.

"Believe it or not, it got me through some tough times," she said. "I just wanted to say…" she paused. "Well, I really don't know what to say to you, except that I want to say something."

"You already have," I said.

"I heard," she said. "I heard some bad things about you."

"You don't have to say anything," I said to her. "I'm glad that I got to see you, but I should be getting back."

The bourbon was gone, leaving only the residue of gasoline in my chest and face and ears. There was no memory anymore. No magic potion.

Outside, the winter was gathering on the fall, the skeletal trees were bare in the light of streetlamps.

You are the silent streets before dawn, the waking moment, a breath of sunlight in golden pearled birdsong. Of wistful afternoons, and windswept meadow grass, the paradise scent of autumn apple paths.

The back door of the bar opened behind me, and for a moment, I heard that loud surge of noise from the party inside. And then silence again. I could smell Andrea even before I turned around. She took me by the lapels of my jacket and pulled her face up to my face, and I looked into those green eyes. She kissed me on the mouth. She led me into the parking lot behind the bar and we kissed again, and I could taste her mouth, and I was lost in her, and the world fell away, and we were free and floating and weightless.

At last, she pulled away. I opened my eyes and I saw that hers were still closed. So, I closed my eyes also and waited, and just let myself be in that beautiful stillness.

"My mother is away," she said in her soft voice. "I want you to come back with me."

I studied her eyelids, and the short spikes of black lashes, the way the bangs of her hair whispered across her forehead, the carefully crafted makeup, the slope of her neck. I touched her face and held her and drank in that perfection.

IT BEGAN WITH a letter, and it was to end with one also.
It didn't take much for me to pack my things for the trip back
to school. I had only brought a small overnight bag for the trip.
My mother and father had decided that they would drive me back
instead of taking the bus. I showered and afterwards went downstairs
for French Toast and coffee. My father was reading his newspaper.

"Something came for you," he said. He was looking over the
eyeglasses that he now needed to wear when he read the newspaper.
"It's upstairs in your room."

I had made my bed before the shower, and now, sitting on top
of the neatly folded blankets, was a large UPS envelope. The return
address was from some hospital in New York City. I took the envelope over to my desk and ripped open the top. A gold Rolex watch
in bubble wrap spilled onto the desk. I reached inside and pulled
out a letter with a small note that was attached by a paperclip.

Dear Brogan,

*It is with great sorrow that I inform you that Jerome has
died from complications due to pneumonia. Before he
passed, he asked that I send you this watch and letter.*

My Condolences, Nurse Amanda Peterson.

I held the watch up to the sunlight. I put the band around my wrist, but of course it was too big. Beneath the small note was the Polaroid picture that we had taken outside of Diane's house: Frank with a bottle of bourbon, me in my stupid yellow t-shirt, and Bogota standing tall and stoic behind us both. The winning ticket from The Naples Dog Track was pinned to piece of paper.

Dear Brogan,

I would have written sooner, but I'm not much for letters, and besides that, you already know the story. Before they threw me in this shithole, I spent a lot of time searching for the answers that you probably have been asking yourself for a long time. I wish that I had them for you. It's sad to leave this life, having only known you for such a short time, and knowing all the great things that are ahead of you. I never knew how Frank's story ended; I am sorry that I won't know yours.

Don't waste this opportunity for what's ahead for you. You are extraordinary. I'm not much with words. So, I will use Frank's. There is music if you listen hard enough, and if you hear it, then dance. And if they tell you not to dance, tell them to go fuck themselves.

Bogota

P.S. The key is for a locker in Penn Station. Shouldn't be hard for a smart little shit like you to figure out what is inside.

I turned the envelope upside down, shook it, and a small key fell onto the desk.

Acknowledgements

I am deeply indebted and grateful for the unwavering support and mentorship of Doris Kearns Goodwin and Dick Goodwin and to my friend and drill sergeant, who made me believe that this was possible, Natalia Earle. I am further indebted to my friend and author, George (Coach) Gallagher for the invaluable and always ready advice, and for every patient hour spent editing and shaping the novel. Author Chris Behrens, for blazing the way, friend and author J. Lee Glassman for the words and the music, Mom and Dad for everything, Bill and Colleen Gibbs, Amanda Skaggs, mentor Mark Massa, S.J., author Dow Mossman for fielding my crazy phone calls, Dana Mulvihill, who was the voice from the ether, John McCormick (hey man), Geoff Maynard for the countless conversations, The Bogota Guys, 186 Woodstock, Marty Sadlemire, Professor Elizabeth Cullinan, Buca's crew, Wequasset crew, Truluck's crew, Prime Catch crew, and to my friend and author John Knowles, who once said to me, "You will find the story." And a special thank you to my partner and believer, Geralyn.

Printed in the USA
CPSIA information can be obtained
at www.ICGtesting.com
JSHW022345291123
52808JS00004B/18